# What's THAT doing there?

# What's THAT doing there?

## A Garfy Book

DAVID WILLERS AND CATE CARUTH

The Book Guild Ltd

First published in Great Britain in 2019 by
The Book Guild Ltd
9 Priory Business Park
Wistow Road, Kibworth
Leicestershire, LE8 0RX
Freephone: 0800 999 2982
www.bookguild.co.uk
Email: info@bookguild.co.uk
Twitter: @bookguild

Typeset in Minion Pro

Printed and bound in Great Britain by CPI Group (UK) Ltd, Croydon, CR0 4YY


ISBN 978 1912575 749


British Library Cataloguing in Publication Data.
A catalogue record for this book is available from the British Library.

*Dedicated to cat lovers everywhere.*

# Contents

| 1 | What's THAT Doing There? | 1 |
| 2 | This is MY Shop | 18 |
| 3 | The Cat-scratch Drama | 38 |
| 4 | The Big Fight | 59 |
| 5 | Car-crazy Cat | 81 |
| 6 | Celebri-cat | 102 |
|   | About Garfy | 120 |

# 1

# What's THAT Doing There?

Garfield Abercrombie Reginald Fergusson was an elegant ginger cat with a white bib and socks and some very smart stripes down his back. He was very proud of those stripes and would spend several hours a day making sure that they were neatly lined up and that every strand of fur was in the right place.

Now, with a name like Garfield Abercrombie Reginald Fergusson, it was inevitable that nobody said his name in full – that would be far too much like hard work – so everyone just called him Garfy.

"It is a little familiar of people," Garfy would always think, "but I suppose I can live with it."

Garfy lived in the city of Ely, in a cosy house roughly halfway between the cathedral and the river. Garfy allowed a human called David to live there too. As long as David was willing to feed him and open the door for him when he wanted to come and go, he didn't mind the company. There was usually a warm lap for him to sit on, too, when he wanted a snooze.

\*\*\*

Garfy liked to be outside to explore the area around his home. In particular, he loved the large open ground on the opposite side of the road. Once, long ago, there used to be a factory there. That was when Garfy was a kitten though and it had long since been pulled down. All that remained were some low brick walls and parts of the stone floor. Over time, grass and other plants had pushed their way up from the ground underneath, so the whole area was like a meadow. Garfy would go there to stroll among the grasses – which stood taller than he was – and to inspect the gaps in the brickwork for mice and other small creatures. He didn't catch many mice but he knew they were there and he didn't want them to get any ideas about disturbing the peace. He would make sure they knew that he was around to keep them at bay.

No one else ever came near this place. Garfy felt it was his own private kingdom and he came almost every day. In the summer he would lie on top of the walls and nap in the sun, and in the winter he would race the length of the field to keep warm. It was bliss.

\*\*\*

One morning, Garfy made his usual morning visit to his private meadow only to find that someone had put up a fence.

"What's THAT doing there?" he asked himself rather crossly.

The fence was tall and made of metal wire in a criss-cross pattern. It wasn't any major difficulty for Garfy to jump up and on to the bar at the top but it was rather inconvenient.

"I hope it isn't here for long," he thought to himself. "I don't want to have to jump over this thing every day just to get in."

"Mind you," he mused, "the view from the top is nice. I can see all the way to the cathedral and…" he stopped abruptly and stared.

From this high viewpoint he could see some people on the far side of the field. They were in bright orange jackets and yellow hats. With them was a large yellow mechanical digger.

"I don't like the look of this," said Garfy. "What are they doing to my field?"

As he sat and watched, one of the people got into

the digger and started the engine. Then, to Garfy's utter horror, the digger cut out a long trench, right across the middle of his personal roaming grounds.

"What do they think they are doing?" he said in some alarm and, in an instant, he was down the other side of the fence and haring across the field to try and make them stop.

\*\*\*

"Hey!" Nicola shouted out. "Look out! There's a cat!" She was leading the team of archaeologists at the field. While they were watching the digger at its work, she happened to glance round.

She pointed at the ginger cat as he raced towards them. Simon, the digger driver, heard her shout and stopped the engine.

Seeing Garfy, who was still some distance off, he grinned. "The engine must have scared him," he remarked. "Don't worry. He won't come near here. He's probably just after a butterfly or…" Then he stopped and stared. Garfy had now reached them and, with a flying leap, had landed on the arm of the digger.

"Well, I'll be a…" Simon said, and climbed out to gaze at the new ornament on his digger.

Garfy was a very smart cat. He knew that people liked cats and would always stop what they were doing if they saw him. People in cars and vans and other machines were always especially careful to stop for him. He had once caused gridlock in the one-way system around Ely, just by washing his paws in the middle of the road.

"No one is going to do any more damage here," he decided firmly and took himself further along the arm, where he thought no one could reach him. Then, with great dignity, he stretched himself out and went to sleep.

\*\*\*

"Now what do we do?" Simon scratched his head.

Nicola gazed up at Garfy, then down at the trench the digger had created and then at the driver. "We have to do the survey today," she declared. "If we don't, they won't be able to start building next month."

"Won't the cat just run away if you start the engine again?" one of the others, a young man called Mike, suggested.

Everyone nodded, thinking that the noise of the digger would scare Garfy off.

So, Simon climbed back in and turned the key. The engine roared into life with an ear-splitting growl.

Garfy flicked his ear irritably at the noise, lifted his head and sat up.

"There he goes," Mike said, pleased that he'd been right, but also enjoying the fun. His job was to shovel earth all day, so seeing the ginger tom take on the digger had been more entertainment than he'd had in weeks.

Garfy turned his head with a slow, deliberate movement and gave the digger driver *such* a look. He fixed the poor fellow with his green, unblinking eyes, and locked him in a gaze that would melt glass.

For a moment or two, Simon tried to ignore him but

then, feeling terribly uncomfortable, he stopped the digger once more.

"I can't," he said, shame-faced. "The cat doesn't like me."

"This is silly," said Nicola. "We can't just stop because of a cat."

"I'll get him," one of the others offered. Her name was Lindy and, in her spare time, she liked climbing mountains. "I'll just hop up and fetch him down."

\*\*\*

Garfy watched with interest as Lindy scrambled out from the cab of the digger and on to the front. She pulled herself on to the flat section where the arm met the cab and, sliding on her bottom so as not to scare him, she came towards him.

"Here kitty, kitty," she said. "Here kitty, kitty."

Garfy flicked both ears, intrigued to see what she'd do next.

As Lindy came within reach, she made a grab for Garfy who, in one effortless bound, leapt onto the roof of the cab.

Lindy sighed and, looking down at the grinning faces of the others, said, "I'll just go up and get him."

"You do that," Mike smirked. He was rather hoping this would go on all morning. He hadn't had so much fun in ages.

Getting on to the top of the digger was harder than reaching Garfy on the bonnet. The sides of the digger were very slippery. Lindy wasn't scared of heights though and all the rock climbing she did meant that her arms were very strong. She pulled herself up and then, carefully, so as not to make Garfy jump, reached out and tickled his cheek.

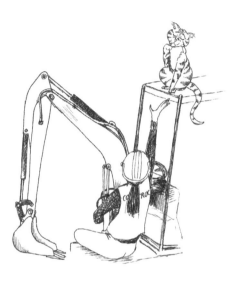

Garfy purred. He liked being made a fuss of.

Lindy beamed down at the others. "There. Now I'll just… Ahhh!" The moment she went to take hold of the cat, he sidestepped her and took another flying leap. This time he landed on the bucket at the very tip of the digger.

"*Right!*" said Lindy, through gritted teeth. "This means *war!*" And she slid back down to the bonnet. Without even thinking about it, she ran up the arm of the digger.

"Here!" Simon cried out. "Watch it. That's not safe."

Lindy took no notice and, to Garfy's great surprise,

reached him on the bucket within seconds and scooped him up before he could react.

"Got him!" she cried. Then, with the cat firmly in her arms, she looked around. "Err…" she said, in puzzlement. "How do I get down?"

*** 

There was nothing Garfy could do but watch in disgust as the digger continued its work – creating a deep trench right through the middle of *his* field. He would have loved to prevent it but Lindy still had him in her arms and she wasn't about to let him go. It was only when Simon had stopped the digger and got down that he was finally released.

"Perfect," said Nicola, and then she and the others all climbed into the trench and began to poke and prod at the sides and make lots of notes.

Garfy continued to watch them, partly to be sure they didn't do any further damage and partly because he was really quite curious as to what they were doing. After a while, he couldn't resist joining them in the trench.

"Come to join the fun?" asked Mike, tickling Garfy's chin with a smile.

Garfy purred briefly. Then, remembering that he wasn't happy about these people being here, he stopped and stalked off to the other end of the trench. There, Nicola and Lindy were talking.

"It doesn't look like there is anything of interest here," Lindy was saying.

"No," Nicola agreed. "If there was any archeology, it would have been destroyed when they built the factory. I guessed that would be case."

"One supermarket coming up, then," said Lindy with a grin.

"Supermarket?" Garfy thought to himself when the ditch had been filled in and everyone had gone home. "I wonder what they mean."

\*\*\*

For the next few weeks all was quiet. The fence was still up around the field – not that that stopped Garfy for a moment – and, once again, the meadow was his to enjoy. Once or twice, people with poles would come and walk across the field and take measurements but that had happened before and they didn't bother Garfy, so he didn't bother them.

Then, one rainy Monday, Garfy sauntered across to the field and stopped dead. The whole area was a seething mass of machines and people, all in yellow jackets, hard hats and green boots. Already the ground was being dug up and piles of bricks and sand were being stacked around the area. In one corner a hut was being built and there was noise and dust and movement everywhere.

"What's all THAT doing here?" he said, aghast.

It was one thing to have a few people digging holes for a day or two but this was quite a different proposition. All this noise and mess and fuss was horrid. From everything that was going on, it was clear that the people were planning on staying for some time and were going to make lots of changes to the meadow.

"No, no, NO!" Garfy declared. "This is MY field and I will NOT allow it to be messed up this way. I am Garfield Abercrombie Reginald Fergusson and this will NOT do!"

He looked on in despair at all the chaos. There didn't seem to be much he could do right this moment and he needed peace and quiet to come up with a plan. He stalked off home and took a nap on the sofa instead.

By the evening, he had an idea. He could make friends with everyone during the day and listen in on their plans. Then, at night, he could do what he could to stop them. People didn't usually work at night – they didn't seem able to see in the dark like he could – so that would be his opportunity to convince them all to leave.

\*\*\*

And that was what he did. During the day, he would walk about the site, say hello to the builders, jump into the vans which brought people and supplies to the site, took naps on the chairs in the hut in the corner of the field and inspected the paperwork on the desk.

Then, at night, he would come back and cause mayhem.

When the builders laid a floor of cement all the way across the field during the day, Garfy spent the night chasing moths across it, completely ruining the surface.

When the builders stacked the tools away neatly at the

end of the day, Garfy would dive into the tool box and rummage around until everything was in a muddle.

When the drivers hung their van keys up on a row of hooks, Garfy would steal them away and drop them into the ditch at the back of the field.

Anything he could do to slow down the building work, he did.

\*\*\*

"I can't understand it," the site manager, Chris, said to her assistant, James, one morning. Work had been delayed for over an hour because all the nuts and bolts and screws had been knocked out of their boxes all over the floor and they all had to be sorted out before work could begin again. "It's as if the site is haunted, with all these tricks and pranks." She stroked Garfy, who was purring contentedly on her knee.

"I know," James replied as he offered Garfy a bit of his fish sandwich. "I would have said it was kids coming in to cause mischief, only the security guards are all on the lookout for things like that. They are sure that no one is making it on to the site at night."

"Hmm," said Chris. "I can't think what it can be. Can you?" And she tickled Garfy behind the ears.

"No idea," James replied as he poured some of his tea into a saucer and put it on the floor for the ginger tom.

\*\*\*

And so it went on. By day, Garfy was the site mascot. At night he was a saboteur, slowing down the building works as best he could. And all the while, Chris was getting more and more worried and cross at the delays in the work.

"If this carries on," she said, "we won't be open until Christmas."

Then, one night, Garfy got too clever for his own good.

Some bags of plaster had been delivered and piled up in one corner of the field. Garfy decided the thick paper bags would be excellent for sharpening his claws.

He was working his way along the pile, pulling and scratching at each bag until they split open and the dry white powder began to pour out on to the damp ground.

It was raining that night – a fine drizzle coming down – and, for each bag that was torn open, the water was soon mixing with the plaster until it was sticky and starting to set.

All of a sudden, a flashlight turned on and flooded the whole area in light – catching Garfy in the act.

"Got you!" said Chris angrily and, on realising that it was Garfy who had been causing all the trouble, stared in disbelief. All this time, she had welcomed Garfy on to the site, allowed him to sit in the hut for warmth, and given him bits of her lunch, and this is how he repaid her – by sabotaging all the hard work they were doing. She made a grab for him.

Garfy was too nimble and, before Chris could lay a hand on him, he was off and running. He went as fast as he could but it wasn't long before he realised that Chris was making no attempt at chasing him. He stopped and watched as she walked across the field, got into her car and drove away.

"That's odd," Garfy thought. "I wonder why?"

He didn't have to wonder for long. When he got home, who did he see, sitting on the sofa with a cup of tea in her hand, but Chris? David, the human he allowed to share his house, was looking rather grave and was nodding.

"We'll keep him in," he promised.

\*\*\*

And that was that. For the next six weeks, Garfy wasn't allowed out at all. David wouldn't open the door, however much Garfy mewed and scratched. All he could do was sit on the windowsill and gaze across at where his field used to be. Day by day, he saw the field being laid with concrete and tarmac and then, almost overnight, a metal frame was put together.

"What's THAT doing there?" Garfy asked himself gloomily. "They are ruining my field."

Around the metal frame, builders began to build the thick walls of the supermarket – two rows of brick with a gap in between – all the way along and around the site. Metre by metre, the huge building began to emerge and there was nothing Garfy could do to prevent it.

"So, that's a supermarket," he thought. "I don't think I'm going to like it."

\*\*\*

One afternoon, as Garfy was sitting on the windowsill, brooding over the supermarket and wishing he could be outside, there was a ring on the doorbell. Garfy took no notice at first but then he heard his name and, always curious, he jumped down and went to peer out into the hallway.

There was Chris, looking harried, and talking earnestly to David.

"We can't get to it without tearing the walls down, and it would get hurt in the process if we tried. Do you think Garfy will come?"

***

It seemed that Garfy wasn't the only cat to have been exploring the building site. A little tabby kitten called Lola had been chasing a fly along the top of the walls. She had missed her step and fallen down into the gap between the two rows of bricks. The walls were now too tall for anyone to lean in and grab her and she was too young and scared to climb into the basket that had been lowered down for her. Lola was now so scared that she was running up and down the length of the walls desperately trying to get out and crying piteously.

Then James had remembered how nimble Garfy was and had suggested that they see if he would be willing to come and rescue the kitten.

Chris, desperate to rescue the little kitten, had come to see if, despite Garfy being banned from the site and confined at home, he would help.

***

Of course he would! Garfy came at once. He jumped up on to the top of the wall and peered down into the gap.

"Are you there?" he called out to Lola. "Can you hear me?"

From the far end of the wall he heard a faint mew. It was very quiet and a long way off.

Garfy ran along the wall, calling as he did, trying to work out where the kitten might be by her replies. Finally, he was close and, with a cry of, "Look out below!", he jumped down into the gap between the bricks.

There was a gasp from the builders who had all gathered to watch and stare at the spectacle.

Then there was a long silence as everyone held their breath, waiting to see if Garfy would ever come out again.

Suddenly, from a little way along the wall, they heard Garfy miaow.

"He's going that way," one of the builders pointed back towards the other corner of the wall.

"He's going fast," one of the others said, hurrying in the direction of the cat's voice.

Garfy continued to miaow as he moved and the crowd continued to follow until they reached the place where the basket had been lowered into the gap.

"Pull the basket up," Chris commanded. "That must be what he wants."

Hastily James and one of the other builders grabbed the rope that was fixed to the basket and pulled it up.

"It's heavy," James declared. "He must be in it."

15

Sure enough, when the basket came over the top of the wall, there was Garfy, covered in cobwebs and dirt and brick dust and, under his paw, was a very tearful-looking Lola.

As soon as she came into the light, "I want my mum," said Lola and she leapt off and ran away in the direction of home.

\*\*\*

After that, Garfy was a hero. The story of how he saved Lola spread like wildfire and before long, a journalist from the local newspaper came calling. He spent a long time talking to David and to everyone at the building site and he took lots of photographs of Garfy.

Everyone seemed to have forgotten that he was the night saboteur who had been disrupting the building of the supermarket. Instead, wherever he went, people wanted to stroke him and cuddle him and give him treats.

"Well, this is nice," thought Garfy. "Perhaps it isn't so bad that there are all these people coming to my field." He stretched himself out along one of the walls, to take a snooze in the sun. "I could get quite used to…" and with a big yawn, he nodded off.

He was so fast asleep that he didn't even hear the two builders when they approached, carrying a window frame to be fitted in the exact spot where Garfy was sleeping.

"Oh bother!" one of them exclaimed. "What's HE doing there?"

# 2

# This is MY Shop

The sun was beaming on the walls of Ely Cathedral, bright and early. It was a perfect September morning and everyone in the town was very excited. The new supermarket was due to open today and a *very important person* was going to come along.

For weeks now, there had been signs around the town and mentions on the radio.

*Coming soon – the new Paterson's Superstore!*
*Opening Saturday!*
*To be opened by a **very famous** VIP*

It was going to be wonderful. There were photographs of shiny floors and shelves stacked with all sorts of good things. There was going to be a coffee shop and a children's play area and a big car park for all the shoppers.

If the adverts were to be believed, it was going to be stupendous!

At the soon-to-be-opened supermarket, everyone had been hard at work getting everything ready. Every floor and wall and shelf and window gleamed. Every day more lorries arrived with pallets loaded with everything that was going to be sold in the superstore.

There was everything from toy cars to t-shirts and from nuts to nappies.

Mr Bennet, the store manager, was very proud of the orderly shelves and the clean floors and the neat rows of checkout stations. He strode around the shop inspecting things and testing that everything looked perfect for the big day.

Now, finally, the time had come. At 10:30 this morning, Paterson's of Ely would open to the world. Mr Bennet was particularly attentive today. He wasn't about to let anything go wrong – especially when there was going to be a **_very famous_** VIP coming. Woe betide a member of staff with a spot on their uniform, or a trolley with a wheel that went the wrong way.

\*\*\*

Outside in the sunshine, a big platform had been erected and there were balloons and bunting everywhere around the store. The name *Paterson's* was in big blue letters across the front of the building and there were people dressed up as the blue and silver Paterson's aeroplane, giving out vouchers for everyone who had arrived to see the grand opening.

It was really crowded and noisy. Just about everyone from the city had come to see what the new supermarket would be like. All the local newspapers had sent photographers and journalists and the presenter from the most popular radio programme was there to interview people and to meet the _**very famous**_ VIP. All three local TV stations had sent cameras and presenters too, and they were busy doing introductory pieces to camera and asking members of the crowd to be interviewed and say how thrilled they were to be there.

Everyone was discussing excitedly who the _**very famous**_ VIP might be – because the people from Paterson's head office weren't saying anything more. They knew that, by keeping it a secret, people were much more likely to come out of sheer curiosity.

The owner of all the Paterson's supermarkets, Mrs Phylis Paterson, was there too. This was an important new supermarket for them and she wanted to give it her support to make sure it was a success from the very first day.

Emma, the regional manager of Paterson's, was looking at her watch anxiously. The _**very famous**_ VIP was due to arrive at exactly 10:30 and could only stay for 30 minutes before going on to another VIP appointment.

"We'd better start on time, Mr Bennet," she muttered nervously. "Is everything ready?"

"Completely," Mr Bennet said confidently. He prided himself on being completely organised and everything being spick and span. "Nothing will go wrong."

\*\*\*

Just as the cathedral clock began to chime the half hour, Mrs Paterson herself came on to the big platform, tapped the microphone to make sure it was on and then spoke in a loud and important voice.

"Good morning, everybody. I am so pleased to be here in Ely to see the opening of another wonderful Paterson's Superstore. Ever since my grandfather opened his first shop in Liverpool, the name of Paterson's has been linked to quality and value. Every new store we open is committed to bringing you the very best of everything in a single convenient place."

Everyone clapped politely and wondered if Mrs Paterson was going to talk for very long. It was very hot out in the sun and they really wanted to know when the _**very famous**_ VIP was going to arrive.

Mrs Paterson carried on talking pleasantly about her family history and the rise of the big blue Paterson supermarket chain. Then, along the road leading up to the car park, a great big black car pulled up. It had tinted windows so no one could see who was inside.

There was a buzz of excitement from the crowd.

"It must be a rock star," one of the crowd said to his wife. "Only rock stars have flashy cars like that."

"Maybe it is that girl from the soap commercials," someone else speculated.

"I'll bet it's that Olympic runner," was another suggestion. "The one who got all the medals last year."

Mrs Paterson had seen the car arrive. She knew that everyone was only really interested in the _**very famous**_ VIP – she was only speaking to fill in time until they arrived.

"But enough about me," she smiled. "It gives me great pleasure to welcome our honoured guest for today who has kindly agreed to open this latest Paterson's Superstore for us.

"Ladies and gentlemen, boys and girls, please give a great big Ely welcome to Mr... Josh... Batt!!!"

There was a little silence from the crowd and then, puzzled, they began to applaud. Josh Batt was a local councillor in Ely. They knew who he was but they didn't think he was **_very famous_** and the only person who thought he was *very important* was Josh Batt.

Still, Ely is a nice city and people are polite, so they gave him a polite welcome as he stepped out of the car in a shiny suit with a gleaming white shirt and bright green tie.

Waving to the crowds, he paused in just the right position for the photographers and film crews to get him at his best. Then he ran up on to the platform, flung his arm around Mrs Paterson, turned her into the face of all the cameras to get a great photo of them together and then spun round to speak into the microphones.

"Well, hello my friends," he began. Josh Batt called everyone *friends* – whether they liked it or not. "What a wonderful day it is. And what a wonderful superstore we have here. I am delighted to have been asked to open the store because, as you know, I have been campaigning tirelessly to make it possible for Paterson's to come to..." he stopped and turned his head to one side, sneezing abruptly.

The crowds muttered at this interruption and then, suddenly, began to laugh.

Josh was a little puzzled but continued with his well-rehearsed speech. "It is of great importance to me that Ely is seen as a city which is worthy of the best of everything. That means bringing more businesses into the area, to provide more jobs and… *Achoo!*" He was caught again.

There was more laughter now. It was very perplexing to Josh. What was so amazing about him sneezing? Feeling rather uncertain, he continued.

"… more choice for the people of this great city. I have been a great advocate of… *Achoo!*"

By now the laughter was drowning out Josh's speech and, unable to understand it, he stopped again. Then he noticed that some of the crowd were pointing at something on the platform a little way behind him. He turned and looked.

There, sitting on the platform, watching everything that was going on, was an elegant ginger cat with a white bib and socks and some very smart stripes down his back.

Josh was alarmed. Through the side of his mouth he hissed, "Shoo!" at the cat.

The cat took no notice and began to wash his face with his paws.

"It's Garfy!" someone in the crowd shouted out – for most of them knew about Ely's most famous cat.

Garfield Abercrombie Reginald Fergusson – Garfy for short – lived in a house a little way from where the supermarket was and he had been a regular visitor while it was being built. He'd even rescued a kitten from the building site. He was something of a local hero.

Josh Batt might not be a ***very famous*** VIP, but Garfy was.

While the crowds were pleased to see the ginger tom, all the important people from Paterson's weren't so pleased.

Mr Bennet, in particular, felt that this sudden intrusion was going to interfere with his carefully orchestrated plans. He got up from his seat on the platform and tried to get rid of Garfy by pushing him with one foot. Garfy took a few steps sideways but he didn't leave.

Instead he strolled across the platform, looked out into the crowd with a pleased look on his face and then walked up to where Josh Batt was standing.

Despite being annoyed, Josh forced a smile and said, "It looks like even the local cats are keen to see this wonderful new superstore." Then he went back to his speech.

"Now, where was I? Ah, yes... I have been a great advocate of bringing Paterson's to Ely and have worked tirelessly to ensure it was possible."

Garfy wound his way around Mr Batt's legs affectionately. The suit Josh was wearing was of the finest silk, and Garfy liked the feel of it. He rubbed his face up and down the silken leg.

"And now I am... ah, ahh, ahhhh..." Josh screwed up his face and threw back his head. "*Achooooo!*" He sneezed very loudly into the microphone.

The speakers all the way around the platform took the sneeze and amplified it. It was so loud that they whistled at the noise. The crowds all gasped in surprise and then roared with laughter. They hadn't had such fun in ages.

From then on, the whole business of opening the supermarket fell into disarray. Josh Batt, who, as you have probably guessed, was allergic to cats, couldn't stop sneezing. His nose and eyes were running, so he couldn't speak properly to read the rest of his speech.

When the people from the press tried to take photographs, Garfy seemed to always be there. Not a single photograph could be taken without an elegant ginger tom being in the picture. The journalists loved it – so they made no effort to get rid of him. They all knew that a cat showing up at the opening ceremony was a far better story than a local politician being here.

Mr Bennet, frustrated by how Garfy was making him look, tried to chase the cat off. Garfy side-stepped him neatly at every turn – nipping under chairs and jumping up on to one of the loudspeaker stands to evade him.

And all the while the crowds were clapping and cheering at seeing Garfy outwit everybody this way.

Embarrassed by all this fuss, Emma said to Josh Batt,

"You'd better cut the ribbon and get the store open. The sooner people are inside and looking round, the sooner they will forget all about this cat nonsense."

Josh nodded through his silk handkerchief, as he mopped his streaming eyes. He sneezed again and then, in a hoarse voice, said, "I am delighted to open this Paterson's Superstore. Ely's latest treasure."

Then, using a big pair of scissors, he tried to cut the ribbon. He was so blinded by his tears, however, that he couldn't see to cut it properly and it took him several attempts to get through it.

As soon as it was done, he retreated into his big black car and drove away. All he wanted to do was get as far away from cats as possible.

\*\*\*

As soon as Josh Batt had moved out of the way, Mr Bennet hit the button to let the glass doors at the front of the shop glide open. They revealed a shiny new escalator to lead people up to the shop floor.

Mr Bennet was expecting the crowds to push forward so that they could get in and see the new shop but they had all stopped and were waiting.

What were they waiting for?

Why, Garfy of course! He was also there and, on seeing the door open, he had stepped forward to see what there was to be seen.

Everyone waited as he sniffed curiously into the open doorway. Then, having satisfied himself that the big shop met with his approval, he went with a jump and a skip to run up the escalator and vanish into the shiny aisles of the supermarket.

Now that Garfy had given his seal of approval, the crowds surged forward, eager to explore.

All the way round the supermarket went Garfy and behind him came the crowds. Wherever Garfy went, they went too. Everyone was delighted to see how the ginger tom inspected everything with care. Anything he seemed to like, people rushed to buy. If it was good enough for Garfy, it was good enough for them. It was wonderful!

*\*\**

Did I say everyone was delighted? Well, maybe not *everyone.* The regional manager, Emma, was embarrassed that the opening had been such a muddle and especially that Mrs Paterson had been there to see it. And Mr Bennet was fuming.

"All that fuss over a cat," he said through gritted teeth. "This is MY shop. I'm not having cats wandering in and out of the place."

"Well, it's MY shop," Mrs Paterson remarked. She seemed remarkably unworried about the way the morning had gone. "And I shouldn't worry about today. In my experience, no one remembers these things after a few days. What matters is what happens from now on. And who knows, maybe a resident cat will bring a few more people in." Then she looked at her watch, muttered something about lunch and left.

"A resident cat?" Mr Bennet said. "Over my dead body. This is MY shop!"

\*\*\*

Poor Mr Bennet! Having seen inside the store and realising how pleased people were to see him there, Garfy decided to make a visit to Paterson's part of his daily routine. Every morning he would show up, just around time for his elevenses, and sit at the bottom of the escalator.

Anyone who came into the shop saw him before they collected their shopping trolleys and anyone who was leaving saw him as they came back with their bags of shopping.

Before long, anyone who went shopping bought a little bag of cat treats and had them ready for Garfy as they left. Garfy began to get quite stout on all those nibbles. He was especially fond of the people who had been to the fish counter and thought to buy fresh fish-bits for him.

When he'd had enough treats and petting, he would head up the escalator into the shop and explore the shelves. Customers would find him curled up on the piles of towels stacked up for sale or sitting behind a tower of tins, peering out through a gap when someone bought baked beans for their tea.

All the customers loved him. They would even phone up the shop to ask if he was there before they came to do their shopping.

Garfy was always very obliging. Anyone who gave him a treat or stroked him got a loud purr. If they were sitting down he would even jump up and sit on their lap for a bit. He made sure he shared himself around though.

"I wouldn't want anyone to feel left out," he told himself.

\*\*\*

The staff thought Garfy was great too. When the store was quiet and they were filling the shelves for the next day, Garfy would come and keep them company. He would ride on the tops of the cages stacked with things to be loaded on shelves, and join them on their coffee breaks. He would sit on the counter in the petrol station, assisting as people came to pay and inspecting anything they bought in the shop.

When the big lorries came with the deliveries, usually in the very early morning, Garfy would be seated on the docking bay, ready to guide them as they reversed into place. Then he would help the warehouse team as they checked the deliveries, making sure everything was counted correctly and matched what was on the paperwork. Garfy was fond of the paperwork. He considered it a particularly cosy place to curl up for a snooze. "I do wish people wouldn't keep pulling it out from underneath me, though," he would muse sleepily every time he was disturbed.

In the coffee shop, the serving team kept a jar of cat treats so that people could buy them and feed Garfy while they had their coffee and there was always a dish of water on the floor in one corner for him. Outside the coffee shop there was a big sign saying, "No Dogs, except guide dogs." One of the team added, "No Cats, except Garfy."

*\*\**

While everyone else was delighted by Garfy and his antics, he was driving Mr Bennet crazy! Every time someone mentioned the cat, the store manager would grind his teeth in frustration. He instructed all his staff that Garfy was not to be encouraged. When he saw the sign in the coffee shop, he tore it up and made them take the cat treats and water away.

At team meetings he repeatedly told everyone that cats were not allowed into any part of the store – under *any* circumstances.

None of this seemed to make any difference. Since everyone else loved Garfy they did very little to discourage him. If Mr Bennet was there, of course, they would shoo Garfy away, but when he wasn't looking, they carried on petting the elegant cat and letting him explore the shelves.

As if sensing the hostility, Garfy began to stalk Mr Bennet and make him even more infuriated.

When Mr Bennet arrived in the morning, Garfy would be sitting in the middle of his parking space, paws in front, with his chin tilted upright as if to say, "Actually, this is MY shop."

When an important visitor came to the new store, there, sitting on the chair in Mr Bennet's office, would be Garfy, cleaning his paws and whiskers as if he was completely at home.

When Mr Bennet made his daily inspection, Garfy would always be there, ready to walk round the store behind him – just out of the store manager's sight. He could never understand why his staff seemed to be so amused at his instructions.

When Mr Bennet left at the end of the day, Garfy would be curled up on the bonnet of his car, enjoying the last of the day's sunlight.

***

One day, however, he went too far. Mr Bennet had been especially busy all morning and hadn't had time for any lunch. Eventually, in the middle of the afternoon, things got a little calmer and, feeling very hungry and a bit harried, he went over to the coffee shop for a bit of peace and quiet, a nice cup of tea and his favourite light meal.

Mr Bennet was very fond of tuna mayonnaise sandwiches on granary bread with tomato and cucumber salad. Paterson's coffee shops always made them fresh to order and they were Mr Bennet's absolute favourite.

He sat down at one of the tables with a deep sigh – he was feeling very tired – and, after a sip of tea, he picked up the sandwich hungrily. Just as he was about to take his first bite, his phone rang. For one second he was tempted to ignore it, but he knew he probably shouldn't. He glanced at the screen, saw that it was the head of marketing from London and knew that he would have to answer.

So, he put down the sandwich, picked up the phone

and walked outside the coffee shop so he didn't disturb the other customers as they had their tea and cakes.

The head of marketing was concerned about some upcoming plans for a Christmas promotion so she talked at some length about what was needed and how every Paterson's shop had to make the same offers at the same time. Mr Bennet listened and agreed and reassured her that the Ely store would be absolutely ready for the seasonal offers. And, having finally satisfied her, he rang off and went back to his table and his sandwich.

As he walked in, who should he see but Garfy?

There, on the table, licking his lips, was the ginger tom. And there was his cup of tea, half drunk, and there was an empty plate where his tuna sandwich – his absolute favourite meal – was supposed to be.

"That *does* it!"

With a bellow of rage Mr Bennet rushed at Garfy and made a grab for him. Garfy saw him coming, however, and, seeing the angry intent on Mr Bennet's face, jumped swiftly down from the table, wove between the legs of all the other customers and ran out of the door.

Mr Bennet went after him in a fury. "I've had enough of that wretched cat," he shouted. Then, to Garfy, "Come here, you little thief."

Garfy shot into the main store, heading along the first of the fruit and vegetable aisles and vaulting over the trays of potatoes, to land on the bananas on the other side. He took a swift right-left jink and headed down past the magazines and birthday cards.

Mr Bennet was hard on his heels, his anger giving him extra speed while Garfy, who was getting quite overweight and unfit from all those treats and cosy spots to snooze, was beginning to get a bit breathless.

"This might be it for me," he gasped to himself and put on an extra spurt, rounding the corner into household items.

That proved to be a mistake for, as he passed by, Mr Bennet caught up a broom from one of the hooks and took a swipe at the fleeing cat.

Garfy yowled as the broom swept him sideways and he took a flying leap upwards. He caught hold of one of the shelves, knocking over bottles of washing-up liquid as he went. One of the bottles burst and spilled bright yellow liquid all over the floor. Mr Bennet couldn't stop in time and slid sideways on the lemon goo. Down he went in a heap.

Standing at one end of the aisle, watching the fun, was one of the store supervisors. She eyed Mr Bennet for a moment and then took hold of her radio microphone. "Clean up on aisle 4 please," she said, trying not to laugh at her boss.

Taking no notice, Mr Bennet was back on his feet in a moment and back after the annoying cat.

Garfy was now nowhere to be seen but Mr Bennet strode angrily up and down every aisle, the broomstick still in his hand, poking under the spaces beneath the shelves and asking everyone he saw, "Have you seen that wretched cat?"

No one had but everyone who saw him followed on behind. Trailing Mr Bennet, with enough of a gap to make sure they didn't get in his way, was a growing crowd. Some thought the sight of the angry store manager was very funny and wanted to see what happened when he caught Garfy; some were concerned that Garfy might come to some harm and wanted to be there to prevent it; others saw all the crowds and just wanted to see what was going on.

Up by the delicatessen counter, the aisles gave way to a more open space. On the right was the counter, in the middle was a big self-service salad bar and, beyond that, were the shelves of fresh eggs. Mr Bennet stamped his way to the end of the area, just up by the eggs. The crowd was going to follow but then one of the women at the front threw out her arm to stop them all and pointed upwards. There, on top of one of the shelves on the left, almost hidden by the golden wrappers of the ginger biscuits, was Garfy. His green eyes were glinting as the hunted cat became the hunter once more.

Mr Bennet hadn't seen him and had walked right past.

As soon as Mr Bennet was ahead of him, Garfy jumped silently down and began to prowl after the furious store manager.

On silent paws he got as close as he could and then, in a deep, menacing tone, he yowled at the top of his voice.

"Miaow!"

Poor Mr Bennet was taken completely by surprise. He jumped in the air and spun around – but in his haste he forgot that he was still holding the broom. He caught it on the edge of one of the shelves and it threw him off balance. Before he could steady himself, he fell sideways into the boxes of eggs.

What a mess!

There were egg shells and boxes and yolks all over the floor – and all over Mr Bennet too.

Garfy felt really rather pleased with himself, so he walked over to where Mr Bennet was lying on the floor to get a better look at the chaos he had caused.

He was so busy feeling smug, however, that he forgot to keep out of reach, and with a roar of anger Mr Bennet grabbed for him and caught him by the scruff of his golden neck.

Garfy struggled and hissed but he couldn't get free and the egg-covered store manager dropped him into one of the cages used to store milk, and slammed the lid shut.

The crowds of people looking on gasped in shock.

Garfy was trapped!

*\*\**

Whether Mr Bennet would really have done something terrible to Garfy we will never know. Just as he took a hold of the cage and began to wheel it in the direction of the warehouse at the back of the store, someone called his name.

Walking briskly up the tinned vegetable aisle was Emma, the regional manager. She was beaming as she came towards him and, before he could say anything, shook Mr Bennet firmly by the hand.

"I just had to come and say congratulations, Bennet," she said. "This branch of Paterson's is the best performing store in the whole country. Mrs Paterson phoned me personally this morning to tell me so. She's never known a new store get such great results."

"It's because of Garfy," Tina, one of the customer service managers, said quickly, pointing at the cat. "Everyone loves him and comes to see him."

"Ah, yes, of course," said Emma, gazing vaguely at the caged cat, who was licking egg off his paws. She opened the door, reached in and tickled him behind the ear. Obligingly, Garfy licked her hand. She smiled and picked him up to give him a cuddle. Garfy began to purr. He knew when to make friends in high places!

"Well, Bennet, it is a stroke of genius. Keep it up."

Mr Bennet gave Garfy a dark look but, knowing he'd been outsmarted, gritted his teeth and pretended to smile. He reached out and stroked Garfy rather reluctantly.

"Oh, and Bennet," Emma went on. "Do try and smarten up. You look a mess and I don't like to see my store managers look so scruffy. It sets a very bad example."

And, with that, she handed Garfy to Mr Bennet, turned and left.

Mr Bennet looked down at the ginger tom in his arms, who was cheerfully licking the smashed egg off his jacket, and muttered, so no one could hear him.

"You may think you've outsmarted me, but this is still MY store."

"That's what you think!" Garfy smiled to himself with a deep purr.

# 3

## The Cat-scratch Drama

Garfield Abercrombie Reginald Fergusson stretched out his elegant sleek body on David's lap. Sitting on the man he allowed to live with him was one of his favourite places to nap, but today he was finding it difficult to get comfortable.

He had spent some time cleaning his perfectly white socks and the very smart stripes down his back. As he tried to sleep, however, he was fighting for space with the newspaper that kept flopping all over his face. The more he tried to move around it to find a spare bit of lap, the more his white socks became grey from the newsprint. "Most undignified," he thought. He'd have to spend more time cleaning now and he had been looking forward to a long snooze.

Then something caught Garfy's eye. Right there on the open page of the newspaper was a picture of his second favourite place to be – Paterson's. But it didn't seem the same as it usually did.

The picture showed the inside of Paterson's Superstore all decked out, ready for the busiest time of the year. There in all the aisles were huge red and green baubles dangling from the ceiling and cardboard cut-outs of huge presents, and there was a snow-covered house in the corner of the children's play area. Paterson's was crammed with boxes of decorations, colourful plastic toys and festive food piled high in every single aisle.

Christmas was coming!

Garfy looked closer. What was all that glittery stuff hanging everywhere? It was festooned in every single aisle, from shelf to shelf. There were boxes stuffed with it too.

"Now," he thought, "this is something I must see." It looked like the best cat toy ever.

Garfy jumped down from the lap that had been so disappointing this morning and decided to seek out adventure at Paterson's Superstore. His nap could wait. What couldn't wait were all the things in the boxes, ready for Garfy to play with. "Let's see what all this fuss is about."

\*\*\*

Paterson's Superstore looked bigger and brighter and shinier than it had ever done.

There was tinsel and glitter and strings of lights in the foyer. There was tinsel and glitter and strings of lights at the counters. There was tinsel and glitter and strings of lights all over the tills at the far end of the shop. There was tinsel and glitter and strings of lights on every shelf of goods. There was tinsel and glitter and strings of lights *everywhere.*

Garfy slowed right down to take it all in.

Christmas for Garfy was turkey tidbits, maybe a bit of sausage or two, and a rather unnerving statue of Father Christmas, with a big white beard, a red suit edged with white fur and a pair of big black boots. Every year it took up the place on the windowsill that Garfy liked to occupy when he looked out on to the world from his home.

The ginger tom was mesmerised. This took Christmas to a whole new level. The sparkle and shine was the most amazing sight he had ever come across.

The supermarket was unusually busy today and Garfy was happy to see so many people piling up their trolleys with the biggest and brightest boxes of toys.

Then something caught his eye. He began to follow a man down an aisle that was the most crowded of all. The man wore very bright red shiny shoes, with thick black laces, one of which had come undone. It was the flapping lace that had Garfy running after him.

The man with the red shoes seemed to be muttering under his breath. "Starts far too early every year… all this nonsense… spend too much money…"

"Oh dear!" thought Garfy. "He doesn't seem very happy at all."

The man continued towards the boxes of tinsel and the shelves of lights, then stopped abruptly right underneath a cheery sign that announced, '*Welcome to Paterson's Superstore. Merry Christmas!'*

"Christmas? What's so merry about Christmas?" he grumbled.

Now, wherever Garfy went, he had the extraordinary knack of being able to cheer people up. Maybe he could do the same for this man, who was clearly unhappy about something. So, he snuck behind him and in between the boxes that held all the silver and gold tinsel. "Oh! This is my favourite!" thought Garfy, distracted, and began to pull at a rather long string of gold tinsel scattered with stars. It was longer than he thought so it kept coming and coming and coming.

He began to paw at the stars as the long string fell on top of him and began to tickle his nose. The elegant cat was enjoying himself and thought he looked rather dashing in his golden robe!

"This will cheer that fellow up," he thought, and he walked round and round in circles, winding more and more of the tinsel around him. Then, when he was festooned in golden stars, he sprung from behind the man, bits of tinsel flying, to present his handsome self for approval. Some of the tinsel dropped off him as he jumped and showered the startled customer with golden strands and stars.

Even though Garfy had done his best, the man was most upset.

"Aah!" he cried. "What is that? What is going on? Who brought a cat into the shop? This is disgraceful!" His shouting alarmed Garfy who slunk to the nearest shop person's legs for cover.

"Oh Garfy! What are you doing?" laughed Tina, the customer services manager, who happened to be standing nearby.

"I'm sorry," she apologised to the man, whose face by now was a deep shade of red. It went nicely with his shoes! "Garfy has become quite a fixture here. He means no harm. He's very friendly really."

The man's face started to turn from red to a very vibrant purple. "He's not friendly at all. He jumped out at me and tried to scratch my eyes out. This is a disgrace! Someone will hear about this!" Off he stormed, still with the tinsel streaming after him, which made him look very silly indeed.

"Think nothing of it, Garfy," comforted Tina, as she untangled him from the golden stars, "but be careful around all these decorations. We don't want you upsetting the customers. Especially that gentleman. Whatever we do," her voice had turned to a whisper, so no one but Garfy could hear, "he is never satisfied." She stroked and cuddled the cat as he purred and rubbed his head against her knee.

\*\*\*

It was a busy time of year, Garfy had to admit. Every day, people poured into Paterson's. The aisles were heaving with customers. Shoppers' trolleys were piled high with food and presents and some families even had two trolleys in a train, one behind the other, stuffed to the brim with toys and food and wrapping paper. It all seemed a bit absurd to Garfy – not that he minded. He knew that humans had always been a bit odd.

Still, there was always someone to make a fuss of him and he was getting lots of extra treats.

"But," he thought, "one can only eat one saucer of meat at a time."

\*\*\*

Paterson's had a large section in the corner built as a play area for children. There was a huge ball pool surrounded by tumble mats, a small climbing frame with a swing and a large bench so the grownups could sit. Garfy liked coming here, as there were lots of children to fuss over him and the odd treat or two from the adults. Whenever he strutted up to the play area, the children would call out, "Oh! Garfy's here, look Mum, the big old ginger cat is here!" Well, *big* and *old* was not quite what the elegant cat had in mind but it didn't matter too much. He got lots of cuddles from his visits.

Now, at this time of year, Garfy could see that the play area was extra special. A little house had been placed in the far corner, made up just like a gingerbread house, with brilliant white snow all over the roof and lights which looked like icicles hanging from the tops of the windows and door. By the side of the door were two huge candy canes and tumbling around them were giant wrapped sweets. Right in front of the house stood a large comfy chair, draped with cosy blankets and trimmed with sparkly lights. And who should be sitting on the chair but Father Christmas himself!

This was what Garfy had come for! There was a long line of children waiting to see Father Christmas, so long, Garfy thought, that it might be a good idea to give a helping hand.

As he walked up to the chair, Father Christmas looked down over his half-moon glasses and through, what seemed to Garfy, a ridiculously large curly white beard, he beamed. "Well, well, well, if it isn't Garfield Abercrombie Reginald Fergusson! Welcome!"

That settled it. Garfy was on the up for sure. News of this famous and very elegant cat had made it to the North Pole! This was his opportunity to really get in on the action! Father Christmas was reaching into the big black bag at his feet and out came a large box of kibble.

"Now children, you have the pleasure of meeting Garfy – one of my extra special helpers."

As the children came up one by one, they fed a few pieces of kibble to Garfy, gave him a long good luck stroke and received a little present from Father Christmas. What a treat – for both Garfy and the children!

\*\*\*

This became the routine for several weeks. Garfy would arrive in the morning and would sit on the arm of Father Christmas' large chair, get fed the tastiest of treats and purr loudly, much to everyone's delight. Because of him, the queue got longer and longer every day. Most of the children didn't mind. They wanted to see the ginger tom as much as they wanted to see Father Christmas, so they waited patiently in line.

One day, however, one of the children, a little boy called Ben, seemed agitated. He was right in the middle of the line and he became more and more cross the longer he had to wait with all the other children. He began being very nasty to the girl in front of him and then elbowed his way further to the front. Soon it was his turn to be seen by Father Christmas and his feline helper.

By now, Ben was hot, bothered and very bad-tempered indeed. Father Christmas and Garfy tried to be nice but it was an uphill struggle. Father Christmas is the kindest person you have ever come across and he smiled, handed Ben a present and said jovially, "Hello young man. Now, what would you like for Christmas?"

What happened next can only be described as shocking. Ben started making demands and being really unfriendly to Father Christmas. "I want a new tablet, I want the latest X-box and I want a top-of-the-range sports bike. But your beard is all scratchy and your coat is too tight. I can see your big fat belly poking out and getting in my way, and your trousers are too short, and you look stupid. I don't think you are the real Father Christmas, and I have been waiting too long in the queue, just to see a silly old man and a mangy old cat!"

Garfy couldn't understand what the boy was talking about. He quite liked Father Christmas' fat belly. It was warm and, although the trousers were a little too short, Garfy thought that his socks were stupendous. And as for *mangy* and *old*? Well, that would not do.

"But," thought Garfy, "perhaps he just needs a little

nudge in the polite direction. Let's see if I can help Father Christmas to win him over."

Garfy rubbed his head up against Ben's arm but he was poked in the eye for that. He tried nuzzling into the boy's chest but that earned him a pulled tail. Giving up, he tried to back away but now Ben had decided that he wanted the cat for Christmas instead.

He made a grab for Garfy and started pinching his ears. "I want this cat!" he cried. "And I want to take him home now!"

Well, we all know that Garfy is a good-natured and loving cat, but enough was enough! He didn't want his eye poked, he didn't want his tail pulled, and he certainly didn't want his ears pinched! Garfy flexed his right paw and swiped. He scratched Ben lightly on the arm – just in self-defence, you understand.

From out of the boy's mouth came the loudest scream. "Arrggh! He scratched me! Stupid cat. Grandad! This horrible dirty old cat just scratched me!"

At the sound of the screams, people came running from all directions and out from among the gathering crowd stepped a big leg, on the end of which was a shiny red shoe. The same man who Garfy had tried to cheer up a few weeks back and had been so cross, was this horrid child's grandad!

"I can't believe this cat is still here, causing mayhem, and abusing poor innocent children!" he growled. "This isn't the last you'll hear about this. Something must be done." And with that, he took Ben by the arm and dragged him out of Paterson's Superstore.

"He didn't even say thank you for the present," thought Garfy.

There was an astonished hush over the crowd as they watched Ben running after his grandad, his present with torn wrapping trailing behind him. The girl who had been in front of him in the queue piped up, "Don't worry Garfy, he's gone now. He can't do any more harm." Everyone agreed. They were rather glad they had both left the shop.

\*\*\*

Garfy continued to help Father Christmas right up until Christmas Eve. Nobody heard or saw Ben and his Grandad, and everyone was relieved, especially Garfy. He didn't want to get anyone in trouble, least of all himself. Father Christmas and everyone at the supermarket were glad of his help.

Everyone except Mr Bennet, the store manager. He still didn't like Garfy being there, although he had to concede that the elegant cat had brought even more people into the Ely Paterson's than ever before. He still saw Garfy as a health and safety hazard who made him look foolish to all the other Paterson's store managers. No matter what he seemed to do, however, Garfy was there every single day.

\*\*\*

Christmas finally arrived. The day was spent quietly in Garfy's house, and that was just the way he liked it. He enjoyed delicious tidbits from David, a rather luxurious afternoon nap, and a jolly hour watching occasional flurries of snow swirl all around the roof of the closed Paterson's Superstore.

***

The day after Christmas was completely different. There was a furore at the supermarket when it opened. Paterson's had received a complaint. About Garfy! It was addressed to Mr Bennet, but word got around very quickly. It said that Garfy was a savage animal and had attacked a poor innocent child. Apparently, the attack had left a scar and if Paterson's didn't do anything to remedy the situation, then they would seek compensation.

Everyone at the supermarket was stunned. They all knew that it couldn't possibly be true but the only person who knew for sure was Father Christmas and he was all the way back at the North Pole. How on Earth could they get in touch with him? It was after Christmas and he wouldn't be seen for another year.

Josh Batt, the local councillor, had been sent a copy of the letter too. He remembered that cat, the one who had embarrassed him at Paterson's opening and had given him such a severe case of sneezes that he had had to cancel two important meetings. Garfy had made him look very bad indeed.

"Well, there is nothing for it," he said to his secretary. "Please inform the supermarket that they are to stop that awful cat coming in. We don't want the whole incident being blown out of proportion. It would reflect badly on Paterson's and, most importantly, on the council."

The decree was made. Garfy was banned immediately from Paterson's Superstore.

\*\*\*

"The shop has no choice," said Mr Bennet in his morning briefing to everyone. "From now on that cat is not to put one paw in here." A muffled whisper went around the room. How were they to stop Garfy – who was quick, agile and superbly good at hiding – from coming in? What were they going to do? Post a guard at the door?

Despite the whisperings and dark looks, Mr Bennet felt pleased. The letter had done him a favour. "That dratted cat gets banned," he thought, "and I didn't even have to do it! Now things can go back to normal without him skulking about and messing up MY shop."

Word spread quickly of Garfy's ban and before long, someone had informed all the local newspapers. The very next day it was headline news:

*Paterson's mascot, Garfy,*
*banned from shop in tragic miscarriage of justice*

read the headline.

The return to normal Mr Bennet had hoped for wasn't to be. He drove into the car park of Paterson's that morning and there, at the front door, were people with banners emblazoned with 'BOYCOTT' and 'UNFAIR TO CATS'.

There was a full demonstration, with placards no less, right in front of Paterson's. *His* Paterson's – the supermarket he had built from the ground up. The supermarket that had been called 'best performing store in the country'. Now people were protesting right outside the doors, shouting and waving their homemade signs.

Mr Bennet cautiously got out of his car and began moving stealthily towards the back entrance, hoping to avoid a confrontation. He needn't have bothered for, just as he moved around several cars so as not to be seen, the crowd started to move off.

"Right," shouted the woman at the front, "off to the Town Hall, and straight outside Mr Batt's window. Let's tell him how disgusted we are at having our dear Garfy banned."

Mr Bennet made it inside Paterson's and, during the trip up the back stairs, he tried to come up with a strategy to avoid any disgruntled shoppers. But again, he needn't have bothered.

Paterson's was deadly quiet. There didn't seem to be any shoppers walking down the aisles, there was no one at any of the counters and the tills were all silent. Mr Bennet grabbed the supervisor from in front of the vegetables.

"What's going on? Why is nobody here? Open the main doors immediately. Let people come in. We are open."

"But," the supervisor said, "there's no one to come in. Paterson's is being boycotted."

It was very quiet in the supermarket all that day. Even Garfy didn't stay very long. He had arrived during the protesters' march and their angry shouts and mentions of cats unnerved him. He left pretty quickly, back to the safety of his home and the lap he shared with the newspaper.

***

The following week things took a different turn when Mrs Paterson herself began to receive letters of complaint. In fact, her desk and her inbox were filling up with mail and they all said the same thing: how unfair it was that Garfy wasn't allowed into Paterson's Superstore any more; how he had actually made the experience of shopping a much brighter one; and now they were thinking of going somewhere else to get their groceries.

Each letter told a different version of the story. Some blamed the little boy, some blamed the angry man with the red shoes, some blamed Mr Bennet and some blamed Josh Batt. In one thing, however, they were agreed: Garfy was the victim of a miscarriage of justice!

Alarmed by what she was hearing, she asked Mr Bennet for a full report on the situation. He, of course, downplayed the fact that the supermarket was very quiet, and blamed it on the post-Christmas lull.

Mrs Paterson wasn't having any of that nonsense. She had been in this business for a long time and she knew that it all sounded a bit fishy to her. If Mr Bennet wasn't going to tell her the truth, then she would pay Ely a visit and find out for herself what was going on, and she'd get that puffed-up councillor to meet her there. He had some explaining to do too.

\*\*\*

As soon as she stepped out of the car in front of the Ely Paterson's, Mrs Paterson spied the elegant ginger cat, sitting at the front door of the supermarket, looking very forlorn.

"Now, now, Mr Fergusson," she said as she approached him. "What trouble have you been causing this time?" She tickled him under the chin.

Garfy recognised the lady as soon as he saw her. She was the one with kind eyes, who seemed to be in charge. "Well," he thought, "if I can win her over, maybe, just maybe, I'll be allowed back into MY shop."

He stretched out his handsome stripes, made sure his white socks were spotless and began purring loudly and melodically as he rubbed up against Mrs Paterson's leg and nuzzled into her stroking hand.

"Oh Mr Fergusson! You are shameful!" Mrs Paterson said, not fooled for an instant by his charm offensive. "Let's see what we can do for a handsome cat, shall we?"

They could both hear Josh Batt, the councillor, before they could see him. He only had to take one look at a cat to start sneezing.

As soon as Garfy saw who it was though, he thought he'd be banned for life if he was there. So, the cat gave Mrs Paterson one last nuzzle and dashed off.

"*Achoo!* Was that the cat all this fuss is over…?" Mr Batt asked.

"No, I don't think so," fibbed Mrs Paterson. She didn't want to make matters worse and certainly wanted to be in charge of this meeting. "No, it wasn't. Some other cat wanting in on the action, I expect."

"Hmm, I'm sure it was," said Mr Batt. He wasn't going to have the wool pulled over his eyes. He'd made a decree and he was sticking by it. That cat was to be banned from this shop and if he came near the councillor again, Garfy would be banned from Ely!

The meeting took place in Mr Bennet's office. The store manager had prepared an even longer report on the incident, although he didn't have any witnesses who could tell them what happened. No one had even visited Ben and his grandad to see if the boy was as seriously injured as was being claimed. It all seemed a bit odd to Mrs Paterson.

Josh Batt sat back in his chair trying to be superior but even he couldn't come up with a valid reason to explain why the story was so one-sided and why he had acted on the strength of a single letter of complaint.

Could they really take this man's story as fact? And was it a good idea to ban a cat who brought in more customers to that one shop than any other in the supermarket's chain? People even came to Ely from miles around to visit Garfy at Paterson's.

Mrs Paterson didn't know what to do for the best but Josh Batt wasn't inclined to change his mind and Mr Bennet certainly wasn't going to help restore Garfy to the shop. She left the supermarket very sad, hoping to see Garfy one last time before she went.

\*\*\*

The news of the meeting and of the ban was spreading like wildfire. It was on the local radio throughout the day, the story made the six o'clock spot on the regional news, and it was all over the internet. The story of Ely's most famous cat had gone viral. (Garfy didn't like the idea of being viral. He had always prided himself on being very clean, thank you very much!)

In no time at all, Garfy was known all around the world. Everyone knew about the cat who had been banned from Paterson's Superstore for attacking children.

Everyone, including Father Christmas.

Oh yes! He remembered the handsome ginger tom in Ely. But the story he was reading in the newspapers was all wrong. Garfy hadn't attacked that child, he was only defending himself against a bully.

What was Father Christmas to do?

Now, of course, Father Christmas can't appear in January – that's against the rules – but he did the next best thing. He wrote letters; one to Mrs Paterson and one to the mayor of Ely, explaining exactly what had happened. Finally, the truth could be told.

As you know, Father Christmas doesn't have to rely on the postal service to get his letters and parcels to their destinations. He has his sleigh and reindeer for that. So, he sent his favourite and best reindeer, Rudolph, to deliver the messages personally, under cover of night.

***

The night the letters were sent, Garfy was sitting at the window, feeling very sorry for himself. It had been two weeks since he had been allowed in HIS shop. He couldn't understand it and didn't know what he'd done to be so unloved.

Wait! What was that streaking across the sky, a red light in front and star-dust trailing behind? Garfy had never seen anything like it! Was it good luck? Was it the wish he was waiting for? It flew so very fast over the supermarket and on across the city that its light disappeared in a flash. Perhaps, Garfy thought, it was all a dream.

***

The next morning, however, he learned that he hadn't been imagining it for, after breakfast, David took him down to the supermarket. There in the foyer was a line of shop assistants and families, all beaming at him. They looked so different from the sad faces he had been seeing behind the glass as he walked past recently. And they were waving to him to come in.

Cautiously, he put a white paw in the door.

Nothing happened. No one shooed him out or tried to scare him away.

He took another step, and another and another. Now everyone was clapping and cheering. "Hooray for Garfy! Garfy is free!"

"What? I'm allowed back in MY shop?" Garfy purred. "Well this is marvellous!"

Father Christmas' letter had done the trick. Mrs Paterson read it with such relief and so did the mayor. All the negative publicity was not only damaging Paterson's Superstore but was terrible for the city too. People had been avoiding Ely since the news broke, not wanting to visit a place which was so unkind to cats. The mayor was able to force Josh Batt to take back his decree and permit Garfy back into the supermarket.

\*\*\*

Garfield Abercrombie Reginald Fergusson pulled himself up to his most elegant height and trotted to the first aisle of the supermarket. He had a long ceremonial train of all sorts of people laughing and dancing behind him. Everyone was so pleased to see the cat back, and they all ignored the scowl coming from Mr Bennet's office window.

As he rounded the pet aisle, the crowd was so large and so jubilant you would have thought that it was Christmas all over again! But when they saw where he was going, they all slowed down and the noise became a quiet hush. All this fuss had made Garfy very tired!

At the end of the aisle were the piles of towels which were Garfy's favourite spot for a snooze. He leapt up into their soft comfort and settled down for a well-deserved nap.

And just as he was about to doze off, he saw in the corner of his eye a little halo of gold tinsel taped to the bottom of the shelf above, and round it the sparkly stars that had so delighted him at Christmas.

# 4

# The Big Fight

It was heading towards spring in Ely, with pots of crocuses and daffodils nodding in the sunshine outside Paterson's Superstore. Garfield Abercrombie Reginald Fergusson – Garfy for short – sat sunning himself in one of the pots, making the most of the warmer weather.

Garfy loved being at the supermarket and he was a huge favourite of the staff. All, that is, except Mr Bennet, of course. Paterson's store manager wished every day that Garfy wouldn't turn up; that maybe he could have one day without that blasted cat showing up.

Garfy was well-loved by most of the shoppers though, Mr Bennet had to admit. They loved to see the elegant ginger tom curled up fast asleep on a pile of towels in the homewares aisle or playing hide and seek with the children close to all the bread and cake stands. Garfy loved humans and really enjoyed being made a fuss of. He always returned the affection he received with purrs and head rubbing and even, occasionally, a hand lick.

And that's what he got every time he visited Paterson's Superstore. The shoppers loved him so much that they often added on to their shopping lists 'Treats for Garfy'. It seemed to the shop assistants that quite a few people didn't come to shop, they came just to see Paterson's resident cat. They would search the aisles to find where Garfy was having a snooze or see him playing with a feathery cat toy that someone had tied to the underside of a shelf. Once they found him, they would make a huge fuss of him, cuddling and stroking him, and then feed him with a few tasty delicacies. Mostly, Garfy entertained one shopper at a time, so no one realised that the ginger tom was getting the same attention from others – fuss, stroke and feed.

Garfy wasn't complaining. He loved David, who shared Garfy's home with him, but the more people stroking him the better, as far as Garfy was concerned.

It seemed to David that Garfy spent more time at Paterson's than he did at home. He seldom made it back for his lunch and David had stopped putting it out for him. That wasn't the only way that Garfy was changing either. It took the elegant cat much more effort to jump onto the sofa, and his collar was becoming so tight that it had had to be loosened three times.

Garfy himself was finding it more and more difficult to clean himself too. Sometimes he couldn't reach his toes to clean them, so his once pure white socks were beginning to look rather grey, and he felt more and more tired in the day. He only just made it to Paterson's, sometimes, without having to stop because he was so out of breath.

Then when he got to the supermarket, he was so sleepy he found it hard to play hide and seek with the children without having to sneak off halfway through for a nap. He wasn't even taking his usual walks around the park behind Paterson's anymore. He was just too tired.

"Oh Garfy! What are we going to do with you?" said David one day. "You're not the cat you used to be. All that attention you're getting from Paterson's is not good for you. You shouldn't be going down there for treats and naps so much. You are looking positively tubby!"

Garfy took no notice. He was loving all the food he received from Paterson's, though he had to admit, he was finding it harder and harder to do some of the other things he enjoyed and there was a definite sideways swing to his middle when he trotted along.

***

One day, after a long snooze on his favourite shelf, Garfy woke to find that it was later than usual and long past his home-time. As he hauled himself to the front door of Paterson's, he heard the birds singing the last song of the day. Garfy sat for a moment listening, his eyes closed.

What greeted him when he opened his eyes again shocked him so much, he leapt much higher into the air than he'd been used to doing of late. There in front of him had appeared a cat!

No, he wasn't looking in a mirror. What Garfy saw was a big, black, long-haired cat, sleek and slim with huge muscly legs and a mean look on his furry face. He started pacing up and down in front of Garfy, glowering at the ginger tom with a menacing look.

Lots of thoughts started whizzing through Garfy's mind, some cross, some scared. "What is he doing here? This is MY shop. What does he want? Is he going to take over? Is he here to be my friend? Does he want to share my favourite shelf?" And then, even worse, "Does he want my treats? Not *my* treats!" The two cats stared at each other. Any passer-by would see, looking at them, that there was no comparison. The black cat looked strong, athletic and healthy. Garfy looked… well… tired and old.

Garfy had to admit he wasn't his usual elegant self at the moment, but the least he could do was be gracious in front of the visitor. He pulled himself up to his tallest height, sucked his belly in and began his introduction and welcome: "I am Garfield Abercrombie Reginald Fergusson, Paterson's resident cat." Garfy tried to stand a little bit taller at this point. He wanted to make what he was about to say next most important. "I have lived here all my life. This is MY shop and over the road is MY home. You are welcome to visit." And then his voice began to waver and became a whisper. "But not for too long."

"Tyson," began the black cat, shortly. "What kind of name is Carpark Abnormal Regiment Furball anyway?"

"It's Garfield Abercrombie Reginald Fergusson!" said Garfy, a little crossly.

"Oh. Whatever. Anyway, what has a cat got to do to get some food around here?"

Garfy was getting a little anxious now. Nothing worried him more than when he thought his food was at risk of being eaten by some other cat.

"Um. I don't know," he said, trying to think of a way to get Tyson to leave. "There isn't much here. You could try further into town. The butcher's shop might have something for you at closing time." And with that, without a second look back, Garfy trotted as quickly as his tired old legs could carry him, back across the road and to the safety of home.

"Phew!" he thought as he settled down to a tea of tuna and kibble. "That was a close one! Maybe he'll find something at the butcher's and be on his way. There can't be two resident cats. It is MY shop after all."

\*\*\*

Little did Garfy know that Tyson had absolutely NO intention of being on his way. He'd been up to the butcher's shop earlier in the day and they had shooed him out as soon as he put the first big black paw inside. He'd wandered around town for a bit, sniffing around bins and in shop doorways for a tasty bite, but he had come up with nothing. Then he saw a big poster in the market place. A poster with a picture of a huge fish on it, declaring:

*Paterson's: the best supermarket in Ely!*

"Yum!" thought Tyson, eyeing the fish hungrily. "That looks like my sort of place."

He loped down the hill that led to Paterson's and there he saw the tired-looking ginger cat lolloping out of the front door. "Easy pickings," he thought as Garfy sat there and then stalked up to him to confront the tubby tom.

As he watched Garfy hurry away after their first meeting, he grinned to himself. "This should be a piece of cake. MY shop, huh? We'll see about that."

\*\*\*

Garfy had a fitful night's sleep after this encounter and dreamed that Tyson was back again, had stolen all his treats and was being cuddled and petted by all the humans, right there at Paterson's front door. Everywhere inside there were toys for Tyson and places set aside for him. That startled the poor ginger cat awake and, before David could get up and give him his breakfast, Garfy had squeezed out through the cat-flap and was heading to the supermarket. "MY shop," he kept muttering as he went, "MY shop... MY SHOP!"

He was out of breath and puffing really hard when he got to Paterson's car park. He had practically run all the way there and was now feeling very dizzy. How did he get this unfit?

To his relief, there was no sign of Tyson anywhere outside. What about inside the shop? Garfy must investigate but, he had to admit, he was a little afraid to step inside. What could he do if Tyson had taken over? What if he'd got there early and now it was HIS shop? Garfy didn't think he had it in him to try to claim it back.

By the time he had reached the row which had his favourite bale of towels at the end, Garfy's heart was beating really hard and fast. As he rounded the corner, he squeezed his eyes tight shut, not wanting to see what he dreaded might be there. Would he see Tyson, curled up in his spot, playing with his cat toy and being fussed and fed by the early morning shoppers?

He crept a little closer, still with his eyes shut. This was a bad decision because as he walked past a new display of the Karen Kollinger Kibble all stacked into a tower, they began to fall one by one, at first slowly and quietly, then quickly crashing all about him and all over the floor. Garfy opened his eyes in fright, no longer worried about looking at the towels as he dashed the rest of the way down the aisle, away from the mountain of boxes coming his way.

And then, all of a sudden, he was there, at his favourite spot. There was no sign of any cat but him! Garfy, his heart nearly coming out of his chest, grinned from ear to furry ear!

"What a silly cat I am! Tyson is long gone!"

He was so glad that the big black cat was nowhere to be seen. He just sat in the middle of the aisle staring into space, his heart slowing down to normal.

The floor manager, Hannah, had come rushing on hearing the commotion and saw the devastation in her area. "Garfy! What do you think you're up to? We spent a long time putting up that display and now half of the boxes are ruined!"

Garfy was sorry he'd made such a mess. He didn't want to upset anyone, least of all people who always took such good care of him. He couldn't think how he had come to knock the tower over. He was sure he didn't touch the display but he hadn't been looking and it had fallen right beside him. It must have been his tail that had knocked it.

Hannah didn't care about that. She was so upset that she shooed Garfy out of the aisle so she could clean up.

As he trotted away into the next aisle, Garfy's heart began pounding faster than ever. Who should come skulking round a pile of tinned vegetables but the big black cat!

Tyson had been there all along. He had the biggest and most pleased-with-himself smile on his face. Garfy knew straight away what that meant. It was Tyson who had knocked over the boxes. Tyson was deliberately trying to get him into trouble. But why? Surely the butcher had given him some food yesterday. Tyson couldn't possibly want food from Paterson's too?

Tyson had indeed knocked over the display and was very pleased with himself about it too. After Garfy had left the night before, he had taken a surreptitious look about the superstore and he very much liked what he saw. A clean place to live, any number of comfy places to sleep, cat toys and all the food he could possibly imagine. With only that tired old cat to deal with, he thought, he'd have the run of the place in no time.

*\*\**

So began Tyson's plan of attack. He would be at Paterson's front door BEFORE it opened, miaowing oh-so-sweetly as staff opened up for the day. By now, all of Paterson's staff were cat lovers thanks to Garfy, and they thought this handsome long-haired cat was a perfect addition to the family.

"Oh look!" said Jack, who ran the deli counter. "He's here again, bright and early! Stop by later and I might have a few tidbits for you." Everyone was really warming to this very good-looking cat, always there and always ready to please.

Because Tyson was fitter, faster and more agile than Garfy, he was always the first to run up to customers as they came into the supermarket and curl his long and glossy tail around their legs. The children thought he was wonderful when he was there waiting for them, just like Garfy used to. Morgan and Isabella, who regularly visited Paterson's (usually in the hope of being bought a triple chocolate banana sundae in the café), thought that Tyson was very handsome and friendly, and he did have the perfect miaow. Garfy would always be their favourite, even though these days he was always trailing behind and seemed to be less interested in being there.

\*\*\*

This was far from the truth. Garfy was starting to regret all those months of being lazy and eating too many treats. David was right. He wasn't the cat he used to be. He was so tired these days that he slept most of the time and missed out on all the cuddles shoppers used to give him. He had become so lazy and hadn't played hide and seek with the children for such a long time that he'd almost forgotten how to play it.

Besides all that, Tyson had muscled his way into the supermarket and into people's hearts.

It seemed that Paterson's had forgotten about Garfy. Maybe it was no longer HIS shop. He was very sad at the thought of it. He miaowed quietly as shoppers passed by and, if they weren't in a hurry, they would quickly pat him and tickle him under his chin. He was still loved but the shoppers had something new on their shopping lists: 'Treats for Tyson'.

Tyson was not satisfied though. He wanted Paterson's to himself. He wanted to say, "This is MY shop". So, his plan went a step further. He decided that he would become invisible, so that anything bad that happened was blamed on the flabby old ginger cat. What's more, Tyson would see to it that bad things *did* happen.

From then on, wherever Garfy went, Tyson was skulking close behind, poised to cause mayhem.

\*\*\*

More boxes went over on Monday – Mr Fry's Flakes spilled their contents all over the cereal aisle.

"Garfy!" shouted Evan, the cereal aisle supervisor. "Shoo!"

On Tuesday, just as Garfy walked through the dairy aisle a whole row of four-pint cartons of milk fell onto the shiny floor that Pete, the cleaner, had just finished mopping.

"Garfy!" he shouted. "Shoo!"

On Wednesday, they found paw prints in the butter and on Thursday all the children's socks had been shredded.

It was all blamed on Garfy and, every time, he was told, "Shoo!"

He had done none of it, of course, but how was he to let people know that it was Tyson when he kept being shooed away so people could clear up?

Friday came and Garfy felt defeated. He knew that Tyson was bigger, fitter and faster than him, so he decided to discuss a truce with the big black cat.

Tyson was there, early as usual, and Garfy tried to talk to the big black cat to make an offer of his second-best comfy spot on top of the newspapers. Just so long as Tyson stayed there, away from him.

But Tyson wasn't prepared to share and carried on making a mess so that Garfy would be blamed.

\*\*\*

Another week passed and, on the next Friday night, as Garfy was on his way out of the supermarket, he was trying to think what to do for the best. He really didn't want any trouble. He was usually a mild-mannered cat and besides, he didn't want to fight Tyson. It was not Garfy's way. These days, however, he didn't always get his way.

As he rounded the corner of the magazine aisle Tyson emerged and blocked Garfy's path. He wanted the lazy ginger cat out of HIS shop!

"What are you still doing here?" he hissed. "I thought you would have got the message by now. THIS IS MY SHOP!"

"I don't want any trouble," said Garfy, trying to get past Tyson.

"Course you don't. You're fat, flabby and out of shape. You couldn't handle trouble."

"I'm happy to share my shop with you," Garfy said timidly.

"Oh, no you don't," Tyson spat at him. He came closer to Garfy. He trod on the ginger tom's tail on purpose, and kept a rear paw there while, with his front paw, he prodded Garfy in the chest. As he jabbed, he spelled it out quite clearly. "YOU. Get. Out. Of. My. Shop. GET OUT OR I WILL THROW YOU OUT!"

Poor Garfy, what was he to do? He had tried so many times in the last few days to make things better but now he was angry. He scratched Tyson on one ear as a warning. He really didn't want this but he felt he had no choice.

As soon as he'd done it though, he wished he hadn't.

Tyson's eyes went red, his fur stood up all over his body and he arched his back, ready to pounce.

Garfy knew he had to get away, and quickly, so he turned and fled but Tyson was a lot faster than him.

Garfy managed to get past the pharmacist's counter before he was caught. Tyson scratched at his back and clobbered him round the head. Again and again the big bully of a cat battered him, scratching at him and pulling out chunks of ginger fur.

Garfy did his best to defend himself and got in a few blows of his own but he was coming off worst by a long way.

As Tyson drew back his paw to strike again, Garfy leapt as far as his tired legs could manage, and he scrambled up the shelves of the pharmacy, pulling down medicines which promised to stop that runny nose and help fight off eyes streaming from hayfever. He reached the last bit of shelving and began pelting down the middle of the top shelf. Tyson was gaining on him, having pushed all the boxes of cough medicine from the top of a cupboard, where they oozed their sticky mess all over the floor.

Tyson snatched at Garfy's tail and Garfy tried to cling on to the only thing that was left on the shelf, a huge bag of cotton-wool balls. They were no help of course. Garfy scratched at the wrapping again and again, until it was in shreds. Then all the cotton-wool balls began to scatter across the empty shelf. There was nothing for it. Garfy grabbed a handful and threw them at Tyson, hoping to knock the big bully off the shelf and away from him.

The cotton-wool balls landed on Tyson with a soft "pumpf". They didn't deter Tyson for a moment. He was still right there, on the top shelf, gripping tightly to Garfy's tail with his front paws.

Then something surprising happened. Tyson began to laugh! He laughed so much he let go of Garfy's tail and staggered backwards a few paces. "You stupid old cat!" he guffawed. "Those things won't hurt me, they're made out of nothing but air." He laughed so hard that he very nearly fell off the shelf all on his own, without the help of cotton-wool balls!

This was Garfy's chance. He was far enough away from Tyson to get a head start. He ran along the top of the shelf, breathing hard, his heart pumping fast. He had never been so tired and worn out but he had to get away. His poor scratched-up body was coming to a stop. He couldn't go on any further. His head was pounding with all the punches it had got from Tyson and his ears and paws were so sore from all the scratches that he couldn't go on.

Garfy had reached the end of the shelf now. It was hot up there and, as he looked at the baby wipes to his left and lotion to the right, he began to feel very dizzy. Everything in Paterson's had suddenly gone out of focus and, as he closed his eyes and fell into a large cage of nappies, the last thing he saw was Tyson leaping at him.

\*\*\*

When David was hastily summoned to Paterson's by Tina, the customer services manager, he was horrified at what he saw. Garfy was wrapped in a towel in Tina's office and was clearly in a bad way. No one could guess what had happened to him. He'd been found in the pharmacy aisle, surrounded by bottles and packets from the emptied shelves.

"He must have fallen," guessed Tina.

David rushed him to the emergency vets, thinking the worst. His poor cat looked so beaten up he didn't think Garfy would ever recover. By the time the vet had finished with him, he had so many bandages wrapped around him that he looked like a mummy!

For the next few days, Garfy lay on the sofa being nursed by David and sleeping as he recovered from his injuries. He was taken to the vet every day to have his dressings changed and to see how he was doing. By the end of the week the vet was satisfied. Garfy was a very lucky cat – he would make a full recovery.

\*\*\*

Back at Paterson's everyone waited for news of Garfy. The night of the fight had been very quiet so no one knew what had happened. All they saw was the mess that had been made and Garfy's poor battered body lying in the wreckage.

Tyson, of course, made himself comfortable at Paterson's, now ruling over his domain. His true nature was beginning to show through though. As the days went on, he became more and more aloof and, despite eating all the treats the shoppers brought him, he never once purred or thanked them in any way. He sat upright on the bale of

74

towels that Garfy had so liked and, even though he had lots of chin tickles and back rubs, he didn't cuddle up to any of the children, who, a few weeks before, had been thinking that he was nicer than sleepy old Garfy.

News was beginning to leak out, too, that the vet's report suggested that Garfy's injuries looked like the result of a fight. What's more, long black hairs had been found caught in one of Garfy's paws.

After a week, Morgan and Isabella were missing Garfy so much that they asked their mum and dad if they could go and see him after they had gone shopping. Mum and Dad agreed – they missed Garfy too. So they rang David, who was pleased that they were going to pay Garfy a visit.

"He needs cheering up," David told them. "He's recovering but he hasn't left the house once. I think he might have lost his confidence."

When she heard that, Isabella asked if Uncle Bruno could come along too. She was hatching a plan for Garfy and she thought that Uncle Bruno was just the man to help a wounded cat.

Morgan and Isabella's uncle owned his own gym. He coached everyone from dancers to boxers. He knew more about getting fit than anyone else in Ely and Isabella was sure he could get Garfy back to being the sleek and elegant cat who was so loved by everyone.

Uncle Bruno took one look at Garfy and announced, "What you need, young pussy-cat, is a fitness regime. We'll get you back fighting fit and ready to take on the world again."

*Young pussy-cat*! Garfy hadn't been called 'young' for ages. Tyson had called him old and fat and flabby for so long, he'd begun to believe he could never be anything different.

At the thought of Tyson, Garfy slunk back into his bed and licked his bandages. He wasn't going back to Paterson's. He had lost, and now he was going to stay at home forever. He sighed a long deep sigh and laid his head on his paws.

Uncle Bruno wasn't having any of THAT nonsense. As soon as Garfy's bandages were off, he was back at Garfy's house, gently pushing him out of the door.

"Now, young pussy-cat," he said, "let's start off nice and gentle and get you back to full fitness. We'll show that big mean cat a thing or two, eh?"

Garfy really did like this man, not because of the promise of having to meet Tyson again, but the fact that he kept calling him a 'young pussy-cat'. If Uncle Bruno believed in Garfy, then Garfy believed in Garfy!

\*\*\*

Over the next few weeks Garfy was subject to a strict routine and, in no time at all, he began to feel more confident. At the gym with Uncle Bruno, he started with running on the treadmill for a few minutes, before he did the rounds of weight machines especially adapted for the *young pussy-cat*! After a gruelling half-an-hour of lifting, he had a sauna and a massage to relax all his aching muscles. He was also on a strict diet of healthy food. No treats for him while he was in training. Uncle Bruno was serious about that: there was to be no slipping off to the nearest cupboard for a sneaky bite of something.

Garfy, unusually for him, stayed true to his training. Morgan made him sweatbands for his head and front paws, and Isabella put together little cat weights, so he could build up his muscles when he wasn't at the gym. He worked hard in the months after the fight with Tyson, until he was, once again, the happy elegant ginger cat with a white bib and socks and some very smart stripes down his back.

***

All the help that Isabella, Morgan and Uncle Bruno gave him, and all the love David showed him, paid off. Garfield Abercrombie Reginald Fergusson had never been fitter, leaner or stronger. He could sprint like the wind and scale a six-foot fence in seconds flat. He was ready to face anything. Even Tyson!

The day came when Garfy padded to the front of Paterson's and stood staring at the door. He was nervous. He imagined it would be impossible to win all his lovely customers over, given that he hadn't been there for a long time, and Tyson had occupied his place.

Back at Paterson's, however, Garfy was shocked. As he walked into the foyer, he saw that people were rushing around more than normal, with scowls and cross looks on their faces. "What's been going on?" he thought.

In Garfy's absence, Tyson had not only been aloof

with all the customers. He got so bored waiting for treats to come that he started to wreak havoc around the shop once more.

Rows of tins would fall off shelves, packets would be torn open and their contents strewn across the floor, cream would be thrown down from the shelves and the contents lapped. But now there was no Garfy to take the blame!

Tyson was so fast, though, that no one could catch him, so these days everyone did their shopping as fast as they could and left just as quickly.

Paterson's was no longer the happy superstore for cat-lovers.

Garfy was back now, however, and it was time to set things right. He would have his customers back. It would be HIS shop again. "This bully will not continue to ruin everything," he determined.

Now Garfy's training began to pay off. He had much more belief in himself now. "Confidence!" he said to himself. Garfy moved slowly and deliberately around the shop looking for Tyson. He tracked the big bully down, lurking behind the towel bale, sitting out of sight just by Garfy's favourite spot!

When he caught sight of Garfy, Tyson didn't recognise him at first. "Oh, no! Not another cat I've got to scare off," he thought. As Garfy got closer, Tyson recognised him at last, but the ginger tom had changed so much! How had Garfy got so fit?

Tyson tried to shrug off the growing worry in his mind. He rose up to meet his approaching opponent. "Oh, it's you, Carpark Furball, whatever your name is. What do you want? Come back for another beating?"

Garfy didn't blink. He fixed Tyson with a firm stare and maintained steady eye contact.

"Listen," Garfy said with a confident air he never knew he had until now. "As I've said all along, I don't want to fight you. I know it's what cats do, but we don't have to." He raised himself up to a great height, and continued, "We Fergussons have very rarely resorted to violence but, as you can see, I am strong and fit again and I will defend MY shop if I have to. You've ruined this place and it's time you left."

Tyson was taken aback. He wasn't used to being spoken to so firmly. Other cats were usually afraid of him and nervous in his presence. He tried not show his worry and fear as he leapt down from the shelf. He looked Garfy straight in the eye, as he had done that very first day when they met. But Garfy was not that flabby old ginger cat any more, and he was no longer scared of Tyson.

Tyson himself noticed that Garfy was, in fact, taller than him, and he was certainly looking stronger and fitter than he was. Being in Paterson's all day every day had made Tyson lazy, just as it had done for Garfy before him. They had both become too used to being brought treats and sleeping, when they should be out prowling the neighbourhood, chasing leaves and keeping fit like generations of Ely's cats.

Tyson dropped his gaze and started to back away slightly and, as he did so, he was met with a pair of legs, dressed in the uniform of Paterson's. It was Hannah.

"We've been having trouble with this one, Garfy," she

said. "I'm glad you're back to reclaim your territory." The floor manager crossed her arms over her blazer and stared down at the mean bully of a cat.

She was so tall and cross-looking to Tyson, he didn't know where to turn first. Garfy came to his rescue. He lightly stood on Tyson's tail, so the black cat was paying full attention to him.

"Leave Paterson's and never come back." That was it. That was all he said. But he said it with such calm determination that Tyson knew he was beaten even before the first hiss of a cat-fight had begun.

He turned quickly, away from the legs of the floor manager and, tugging to free his tail, shot across the supermarket floor to the exit and was never seen again.

All the customers, including two very proud children, Morgan and Isabella, gathered round the elegant cat and cheered for his safe return. They were so glad to see Garfy back, and looking so wonderful. He was playful and happy again, and that made everyone else at Paterson's happy again too.

And I bet you, if he was honest, even Mr Bennet would say he was glad that Garfield was back. Anything was better than the mean bully of an animal that was Tyson. But I don't think he would tell anyone that, do you?

# 5

# Car-crazy Cat

Summer came bright and early to Ely. All the spring blossom had faded on the trees down by the river, and the leaves had started to unfurl into great green flags that waved their hello to passers-by. The roses in the big plant pots outside Paterson's front doors were in full bloom, and the sun shone hotly over the city.

Garfield Abercrombie Reginald Fergusson loved to stretch out his elegant, sleek body in the shade of the car park on the hottest of days. In the summer it was his favourite place to be. Not only was it cool but he got to greet all the people going into Paterson's to do their shopping. The children would stop and stroke him and the adults would often leave him a treat or two.

Everyone who worked at Paterson's Superstore loved having Garfy around. He had become quite the fixture and he was given first priority in everything. If Garfy was lounging in the middle of an aisle, Pete, the cleaner, would sweep round him and come back later. If he was asleep on one of the shelves, shoppers would tiptoe round and *shush* everyone who went by. Customers even thought it was fun when Garfy sat in the middle of the zebra crossing right outside the front door, cleaning his face. All the cars would line up patiently until Garfy decided he would move and let them pass.

"What's the hold up?" children would ask from the back seat of their cars. "Garfy's on the crossing again," would come the answer. "He won't be long."

Everything was all right in the world when Garfy was about, wherever he was. When he wanted a change of scenery from the car park, he would pay a special visit to the petrol station next to the supermarket. He would slink through the door that was always ajar and leap on to the high chairs in the booth.

There he could see all the comings and goings of the cars on their way in and out: the strange pipe that went into the belly of the car, the hissing snake that attached its mouth to the tyres, and the beep-beep of the machines inside the booth. Garfy could sit and watch forever. He became so curious that he took to sitting outside the booth so he could get a closer look at what was going on.

One day, a big red car pulled up and a shopper got out in a rush, quickly undid the petrol cap and lifted the hose to the tank. She was tapping her hand on her leg, as if she was trying to speed things up.

"She must be late for something," thought Garfy. "I wonder if I can help." He trotted over to the car and the in-a-hurry shopper, whose name was Jenny. As he approached, her face, which was creased in concentration, suddenly broke out into a big smile.

"Oh Garfy! It's you!" she said. "Got to fill up today and I need to hurry. I've got to pick up my children in ten minutes." As the pump clicked and she tightened the petrol cap back onto the car, she gave Garfy a very quick ruffle on the head and dashed off to the booth to pay the assistant.

"Hmph," thought Garfy, as he watched her go. "Not even enough time to stroke me properly." But as he turned around, he saw that in her hurry, Jenny had left the door of her car open.

Now this was an opportunity not to be missed! Without so much as a second look, Garfy leapt on to the front seat of the car. What a sight met his eyes! There was a black round wheel in front of where he was sitting, with long levers coming out of the back of it. What could all these possibly do?

He soon found out!

He leaned on the left lever and a light flashed, along with a clicking sound from somewhere in the dashboard. He leaned on the right lever and out shot bubbly water all over the windscreen. This made Garfy jump in the seat, but when two long arms screeched across the glass he scrambled with such shock to the back seat that he knocked over a metal cup and out spilled coffee into the footwell.

"Ha!" thought Garfy, inspecting the coffee and deciding he'd rather not drink it. "This is fun!"

He returned to the front seat to find out what else he could do. He could see that behind the wheel there were little red, green and orange pictures glowing at him. He pushed his head forward through the gaps in the wheel to take a closer look, putting his paws on the centre of the wheel to keep his balance. A loud 'HONK!' came out of nowhere and announced itself in great waves across the petrol station.

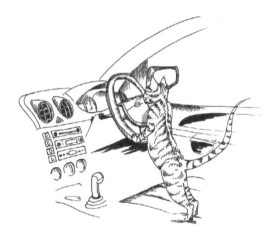

Jenny had just started out of the booth and the noise gave her such a fright, her knees buckled and she nearly fell to the floor. She grabbed at the newspaper stand to regain her balance and then carried on walking, with as much dignity as she could muster, back to the open door of her car.

As she rounded her open door she was met with the cheekiest looking cat with a pleased look on his striped ginger face.

"Garfy! It was you! You naughty thing! Now out you come. I've got to get on." With that, she gently nudged him off her seat and out of the car.

***

After that, Garfy was hooked! What great fun was to be had in these exciting cars of all shapes and sizes! He now shared his time between Paterson's supermarket car park and the petrol station. Whenever he had the opportunity, he would bound through any open car door and explore the inside. He wanted to know what all the knobs and sticks and buttons did.

This one turned the lights on outside. Wow! They were bright and shone straight into Paterson's foyer. This one sent music floating out of the doors, round and round Garfy's head. And this one, well, this one was the best: '*HONK*!' it went and made everyone jump, every time! But then people would laugh, and he would be stroked and tickled. He was hardly ever told off.

On one occasion though, Garfy had more time than usual to explore a large silver van and decided to go beyond the driver's seat and into the very back. There, beyond the shopping, he found lots of tools and packets of seeds and big bags of something he couldn't quite identify. He scratched a little at the cover and discovered that it was a rather stinky lot of manure, ready to be spread on somebody's roses.

"Yuck!" thought Garfy and tried to find something to wipe his paws on. He couldn't possibly go around with this disgusting smell coming from him! Before he could find anything, however, the front door had slammed and the truck was moving off!

"Even better!" he thought. "Now I get to have a ride around the car park too!"

Garfy was so pleased to be getting a lift, he wanted to

thank the owner of the van. So, he jumped forward, away from the foul-smelling manure, through the mountain of bread and vegetables packed in Paterson's bags and straight onto the driver's lap with a plop.

"AH!" shouted the driver. "Wha…?" His van came to a screeching halt just in front of the zebra crossing on which Garfy liked to wash his face. In some confusion, the driver opened his door, and Garfy leapt back into the car park.

"Much obliged!" he miaowed, as the man drove off with a baffled look on his face.

"Well," Garfy smiled to himself, "I enjoyed that!"

\*\*\*

Garfy now had a taste for car rides! Not just any old cars, either!

"I am Garfield Abercrombie Reginald Fergusson after all," he said, "and I rather like a clean and well-looked-after car!"

The nippy little cars that came careering into the car park at break-neck speed were too pokey and the seats were too hard and too small. Garfy couldn't stretch out as luxuriously in them as he could in bigger cars. The medium-sized cars with big long boots in the back were better and they did have lots of room for him to curl up and have a quick nap. They had lots of children's toys and crumbs and sticky patches on the windows though, so he learned to inspect them carefully before he sat down. Sweet wrappers were very hard to clean off once they were stuck to his fur.

His favourite car of all was the first one he had explored. Jenny's red saloon had comfy seats and, even though Jenny had two girls, Millie and Abbie, they were old enough not to make a mess. The girls soon became firm friends of the ginger tom and were always ready to open the door for him to let him in.

\*\*\*

There were times, though, when there weren't many cars around and Garfy struggled to find one he could use to get a ride. Until, that is, he had an inspiration.

He would walk to the far end of the car park, just by the entrance, and wait for someone to arrive. Then, as they drove round the corner, he would get up and limp across the road in front of them. Usually, the driver would know him and would stop to pick him up and drive him up to the Paterson's door, concerned that he'd hurt himself.

One day, however, someone who didn't know him saw this and drove him over to the local vets instead. There he was checked over, given a full bill of health and sent on his way. Poor Garfy had to walk all the way back home.

"Most undignified!" he thought grumpily.

He'd had a lovely long ride in the car though, so it didn't deter him and his schemes became even more daring.

On the day after a sudden summer downpour, Garfy headed to Paterson's via the local park. There, a large puddle had appeared on the edge of the surrounding trees. Garfy waded into the puddle and rolled around in it. He knew that, if he made himself look like a stray, he could get another ride to the vets.

What he didn't expect was that a driver who saw him would pick him up and take him to the cat shelter, miles away. Luckily for Garfy, he had an information chip so the cat shelter was able to identify him.

Lucky for Garfy but not so lucky for David, who had to come and collect him. By now, David was getting wise to the cat's tricks and he wasn't pleased.

"Garfy!" he said. "What have you been up to this time?"

By now, of course, Garfy had been washed and dried and his handsome ginger coat was bright and shiny. No one could possibly mistake this sleek fellow for a hungry stray. David simply couldn't work out how he had ended up at the cat shelter in the first place.

\*\*\*

"No more car rides!" David instructed, but the coolness of the cars in the shade of the car park, the comfy long back seats he could stretch out on and the promise of a ride round kept getting Garfy into trouble.

By now, the regular shoppers who drove into the car park to shop at Paterson's had been warned about the cheeky ginger cat trying to hitch a lift and were on the alert. They would stand guard at their open doors and, if Garfy tried to sneak in, they would catch him and take him to the supermarket front door before returning to their car full of shopping. And so, although he tried every trick he could think of, Garfy simply couldn't get a ride in any car.

Garfy was most put out. He never did any harm to the cars. Why couldn't he have a little fun?

Then, on his way to Paterson's early one morning, something caught his eye. Well, more his ear. There was a loud BEEP! BEEP! BEEP! coming from the side door of Paterson's Superstore and, as Garfy came closer to the car park, he saw a huge lorry with a trailer on the back, reversing up to the door.

This was a delivery truck with a picture of a very large fish on the side, ready to make the day's deliveries of haddock and salmon and cod and prawns. Garfy couldn't resist investigating further. He loved the look of that big fish. As he got closer, the smell from the back, where both doors were swung wide open, was delicious!

There were lots of people busy getting trollies full of fish in ice out of the back, so Garfield decided to nip in at the front. The cab door of the lorry was open and up he clambered. What a sight!

Everything in the cab was so much bigger than the cars he had been in. The steering wheel was so huge that Garfy couldn't see above it. There were many more buttons and levers too and he began to wonder whether this was a car for giants! He made his way behind the driver's seat, where he found a narrow bed which was all made up with a blue duvet and a pillow.

"All ready for a lovely nap," thought Garfy. He couldn't resist it. The smell of the fish was wonderful and the cab was warm and inviting, so he pummelled the pillow to make sure it was extra comfortable, walked three times around the top of the duvet and settled down for a quick snooze. "I'll have 40 winks and then I'll see if there are any leftovers of fish going spare," he smiled to himself.

The ginger tom was so tired, however, that he fell fast asleep. He didn't hear the back doors of the lorry slam. He didn't hear the driver get into the cab and start the engine and he certainly didn't hear the sound of the horn that blasted a '*cheerio!*' as it left the loading bay of the supermarket.

Where on Earth was the lorry going and what would poor David think about how far he would have to come to get his car-crazy cat?

***

When Garfy woke, he was very surprised and also rather pleased. They were driving down a very big road with ripening wheat to the left and sheep grazing in the fields to the right. It was cool in the cab now and the driver was singing along to the music coming from the radio. She hadn't noticed Garfy when she got into the cab. Garfy decided that he didn't want to be noticed now either. If the driver saw him on her bed, she would stop and turf him out for sure. So, the elegant ginger cat stayed very still and tried not to breathe too hard.

He loved being this high up. He could see everything: all the cars going by, the sun shining in through the windscreen and the birds floating and diving above them.

It wasn't long before the driver was turning off the main

road though, manoeuvring the lorry into a long parking space. Garfy lay still until she got out and went around to the back to check the doors and stretch her legs. Garfy stayed as low as his body would let him and slunk through the cab and then down the metal steps to the ground. What he saw and smelled and heard amazed him.

There were gulls screaming in the sky above, the smell of fish (and maybe chips?) was now so powerful that it made him lick his lips in hunger and he heard, just beyond some huts, the crashing of waves on the shore. Garfy was at the seaside!

"What an adventure!" thought Garfy. He hadn't been too far out of Ely until now and the thought of being by the sea was very exciting.

Without a thought for home, Garfy decided he would go and investigate. He was hungry now and the smell of hot fish was making his stomach rumble very loudly.

Garfy followed his nose. The scent of fish and chips quickly led him to the seafront.

All along the promenade walked adults, children running in and out of their legs with huge lollipops in their sticky hands. There were benches all facing the sea, with people sitting to take in the sights or to eat their lunches and maybe an ice-cream or two. The fish and chip seller was doing a roaring trade – the queue was snaking along the promenade and back up towards the car park. The ice cream van was the same – excited children jumping up and down, asking for the largest cone with strawberry sauce all over, please! That queue stretched the other way, up towards the bandstand on the green.

Garfy thought this was wonderful. So many people and endless space to wander in. He was in his element, but his stomach was making very loud noises by now. It was time to find lunch. As he walked past one of the benches, a little girl with a big paper package on her lap called, "Hey kitty, kitty!"

Garfy turned and saw she was waving a morsel of something towards him. Garfy moved closer to investigate. Ooh! Fish! She put it on the floor in front of her feet.

"Slightly undignified," he mused. He much preferred a china dish. He was too hungry to be fussy, though, so he gobbled it down. "Delicious!" he miaowed, and immediately she placed a few more scraps down for him.

Garfy was partial to fish, of course – this tasted like haddock, which was his favourite – but the chips? "Hmm, not so tasty, but bearable."

He was very grateful he was being fed. The sun was shining on his thick ginger fur, making him feel sleepy again, and he certainly needed this food to keep up his strength so he could get back to the lorry for the return journey.

Garfy thanked the girl for sharing her lunch by curling his tail around her leg and stroking his head on her knee. There was so much to do at the seaside, though, so he thought he'd better be moving on to see all the sights. Now, which way to go first?

"Hello!" said a voice from behind him. Garfy turned and got the shock of his life! There in front of him stood a long-haired black cat, just like…

"You look scared to death mate, are you alright?"

Garfy gazed at the black cat. No, this wasn't Tyson. She was a queen, rather than a tom, for a start. She did have the same long black fur, but she had raggedy ears and was rather untidy. She had a friendly smile and Garfy started to breathe again.

"Looks like you've seen a ghost," said the scruffy cat.

"No, not a ghost, just a memory." Garfield drew himself up to his fullest height, just like he did every time he introduced himself.

"My name is Garfield Abercrombie Reginald Fergusson. Pleased to make your acquaintance."

"Mine's Frances, but most humans call me Salty. Salty the seaside cat."

"Most humans call me Garfy," said Garfy.

"Sounds better than the long posh name," said Salty.

"I'm used to it now."

"Where are you from?"

"Ely, near my shop Paterson's, you know?"

"Never heard of it. Is it far?"

"I have no idea." Garfy hadn't thought of it before. He'd assumed it was a fair distance away, since it was morning when they left and lunchtime by the time the lorry stopped at the coast, but he was disappointed that his fame hadn't reached this far.

"Well," said Salty, "that's no matter. What you need is a thorough tour of the place. If you're looking for a guide, I'm your cat."

"Splendid," said Garfy, cheering up at once. "Lead on."

\*\*\*

The afternoon was spent dodging in and out of people's legs as they walked the promenade, lounging outside the restaurant on the green, waiting for food to be dropped off plates, and a very leisurely hour sat listening to the brass band playing wonderful music on the bandstand. They ate bits of fish, chips (still not Garfy's favourite) and a half-eaten slice of bread slathered with butter. They both licked an abandoned and very sticky lolly and chased away marauding gulls as they fought for a slice of cake that had fallen out of a picnic basket.

Along the promenade they dived in and out of shops, some owners calling to them with scraps and a friendly scratch under their chins. Others drove them away with a broom or a rolled-up newspaper, too slow for the wily cats. Garfy loved running through the town with Salty. He felt like a kitten again.

"Time for one last treat," said Salty as she headed towards the van parked on the seafront. "It's closing up time, and there's always a bit of leftover ice cream she's willing to give away to two smart-looking cats!"

Garfy had really taken a shine to his new friend, even if Salty considered herself as smart as Garfy. Mind you, the ginger tom now looked as scruffy as Salty after a day of scouting around the seaside town.

They walked to the van and, as soon as she saw the black, the owner called, "Salty! Good to see you! And you've found a friend too. I was just about to leave. I thought you'd forgotten about me!" She disappeared into the van and returned with two plastic tubs, each with a small dome of ice cream piled in it.

"The perfect end to a perfect day," said Garfy, as Salty miaowed her thanks.

***

The sun was setting as they finished off their ice creams. Garfy began to yawn. "Thanks so much, Salty, for showing me the sights. I guess I'd better get going now. The lorry will want to get off back home and I need to get in without being seen before it leaves." With that the cats bumped paws and went their separate ways.

When Garfy got to the car park, however, he couldn't see the lorry he'd come in anywhere. There were still a few vehicles around but none with the picture of the big fish on the side. Garfy ran up and down the car park, looking left and right, willing the lorry to appear somewhere, wanting it to drive around the corner and wait for him to jump in. He didn't care if the driver saw him now. He just wanted to get home.

How *was* he going to get home? And what on *Earth* was David going to say when he didn't return for his supper?

\*\*\*

By the time it was dark, Garfy was really worried. He guessed that the lorry had gone home without him but he was now so tired he couldn't think what else to do. He had searched the car park ten times over and the only thing left for him was to find a sheltered spot and curl up to sleep. The morning might bring a solution.

But sunrise didn't bring any immediate answers. Garfy was extremely hungry and very tired. The crashing of the waves on the shore all night had kept waking him up. He was used to the quiet nights of Ely, curled up in his bed, all cosy and warm. Here at the seaside the wind had got up and there was no real shelter in the car park.

As it began to fill with cars during the morning, Garfy tried, as he did in Paterson's car park, to get into the back of some of the cars to get a lift home. None of the families were familiar to him though and they didn't know Garfy either, so they shooed him away. Some gave him a few treats out of their picnic baskets but none let him into their car, even for shelter.

Exhausted and a little shaky, Garfy set off towards the promenade, trying to think what he could do to get home and wondering where he could go to get a spot of breakfast. The shops were open now and the music from the fairground at the end of the seafront was in full swing.

Garfy was so shaken by the idea of being stranded here, however, that he'd lost his nerve. Without company he lacked the confidence to convince anyone to give him something to eat. It wasn't like Ely, where everyone knew him. He was a stranger in a strange land and he was beginning to feel very lonely.

"Well, hello!" called a familiar feline voice. "You still here?" It was Salty!

"Oh Salty!" said Garfy. "I missed the lorry and now I can't get home!"

"In that case, you can stay with me on the boat!"

Garfy was intrigued. He quite fancied himself as the first mate on a seafaring ship!

When Garfy saw Salty's home, however, it wasn't quite the ship he'd imagined. The boat was firmly on the ground for one thing. It had a huge hole at the front and was almost upturned. What a wreck! The boat was in the fairground, right in the middle of a crazy golf course. People who came to play would have to guide their golf balls around the boat to putt through to the windmill. The shipwreck wasn't much but, by now, Garfy was grateful for any shelter and particularly for Salty's company.

The days with Salty were spent scouting for food and the nights spent under the tarpaulin of the boat, on two scruffy but very comfortable cushions.

Often Garfy couldn't sleep for wanting to go home to David's cosy lap in a warm house. It had been three days since he left Ely – or was it four? He wondered whether a new cat had taken his place. Had the shoppers at Paterson's forgotten about him? What was David thinking? Would they ever forgive him for running away?

*\*\**

Back in Ely, Garfy was far from forgotten. On the first day when he didn't appear at Paterson's at his usual time, everyone just thought he was resting at home. When David came down to fetch him for his supper and couldn't find him, though, people began to get worried.

By the second day it was all around the city, and by the third, the news had spread clear across the county. Everyone searched in gardens and sheds for the missing cat. All Garfy's friends made posters and put them up around Ely, and Jenny, who knew about these things, posted videos and photos on Facebook and Twitter.

*\*\**

The summer holidays had just begun. Garfy was still missing so Jenny decided to take her two girls on a day trip to cheer them up.

She rushed around, trying to squeeze a few more sandwiches into the picnic basket, and then they all climbed into Jenny's red car. They were off to the seaside!

In the car they too went past wheat fields and sheep grazing, just as Garfy had done before them. The car ate up the miles and, before they knew it, they were parking in the same car park where Garfy had caught his first whiff of fish and chips.

Jenny led the way to the seafront and, although they hadn't forgotten about Garfy, the girls were so very pleased to be at the beach. The fish and chip shop was open, ready to take orders, while the queue outside grew. The ice cream van had arrived and the fairground's lights were twinkling their welcome to the children as they ran on to the sand.

What to do first! Was it too early for ice cream? How big could they build a sandcastle before they had to go? Would Jenny buy them fish and chips for tea?

Before these questions could be answered though, Jenny stopped in her tracks, staring up the promenade with her mouth open. She pointed to a spot just beyond the last row of benches. Abbie and Millie followed the line of her finger with their gaze and who should they see sauntering up the beach with a friend in tow, but an elegant ginger cat with a white bib and socks and some very smart stripes down his back.

Garfy!

The girls ran as fast as they could to where the two cats were walking. Garfy, recognising them immediately, began miaowing loudly and rolled on the ground so they could rub his tummy. He was *so* pleased to see them!

"Garfy! What on earth are you doing here? And who is your lovely friend? We've been so worried. Everyone in Ely is looking for you."

\*\*\*

For the rest of the day, the girls played with Garfy and Salty on the beach, building an enormous sandcastle, sharing their picnic lunch (tuna sandwiches, Garfy's favourite!) and sharing a big ice cream with strawberry sauce *and* a chocolate finger.

Then, all too soon, it was time to go home. Jenny gathered all their belongings together. "Garfy," she said, "you must come home with us. David is worried sick." Garfy turned to his friend.

"Salty, you've been so good to me. Come back for a visit. I'll show you the sights of Ely. There are always plenty of treats to go around and a warm corner to fall asleep in."

"I can't ignore the call of the sea," Salty declared, "and a captain never abandons her ship, but thanks. Come and visit again soon."

And with that, the black cat sauntered off towards the crazy golf and her shipwreck of a home. Garfy was going to miss his seaside friend.

\*\*\*

The trip home was a delight. Garfy sat in the window of the car and couldn't believe his luck. This had always been his favourite car and now he was able to see the countryside whizz by or snooze on one or other of the girls' laps – whichever he most fancied.

Before long they were home, where David was waiting impatiently at the window.

"Oh, Garfy, I've been so worried." He wasn't even cross. He bundled Garfy into his arms and took him inside.

Garfy was looking forward to a full meal and a long warm sleep but he inspected his home with care before he did. It was familiar but it seemed such a long time since he'd been here. And what was that magazine on the sofa? Garfy examined it closely and then let out a little yelp of joy.

David was planning a trip… to the seaside!

# 6

## Celebri-cat

Garfy was famous! The local newspaper was running regular articles about him and everyone loved to hear about his adventures.

FLY TIMES

GARFY WITH ABBIE AND MILLIE....

It had all started with his daring rescue of the trapped kitten at the building site and then, of course, his appearance at the Paterson's grand opening. The drama of the 'banning incident' and Garfy's terrible fight had raised his profile even further. Then, when a photograph appeared on the front page of the Ely Times, showing Garfy on the beach with Abbie and Mille in front of a sandcastle with ice-cream on his whiskers, the story was no longer confined to Ely alone.

The local TV station phoned David one morning. They said they would like to do a feature on Garfy and would David mind if a camera crew came tomorrow to interview them? David rushed around all that afternoon getting everything tidied up. The place was dusted from top to bottom and the vacuum cleaner was on for what seemed like hours. Even Garfy's bed didn't escape the clean up. His cushion was plumped and straightened five times! The house hadn't been a mess before but now the place positively sparkled. "I could get used to this," thought Garfy.

The interview was a great success and Garfy entertained the reporter so much that the crew stayed there for three hours getting to know him. They all took it in turns to stroke him and rub him under his chin. Even the camerawoman, who was supposed to stay behind the camera at all times, couldn't resist Garfy.

The story of Garfield Abercrombie Reginald Fergusson began to spread far and wide. It went beyond the local newspaper and news channel. Soon the national newspapers and television stations were picking up the adventures of the cat from Ely. His picture, groomed and looking fabulous, was on the front cover of *Tide Magazine,* one of the bestselling magazines in the world!

After that, tourists and travellers from all over the world came to Ely. They didn't care about Oliver Cromwell's house or the beautiful walks down by the river or even the cathedral. No, as soon as they got off the train they would head straight to Paterson's to get their picture taken with Garfy.

Even Mr Bennet, the store manager, felt more inclined to like Garfy when he saw how many customers Paterson's had seen that month, all keen to get a glimpse of the famous elegant ginger cat.

Garfy loved every minute of it! He had never been so fussed and cuddled. People from as far away as Japan, America and Australia came to see him as part of their coach tours around Britain. There were pictures of him everywhere: from selfies on social media to huge posters on the side of buses advertising Paterson's Superstores. He felt very famous and very proud of himself.

Garfy's next step into stardom came when David received a phone call from the most prestigious cat show committee. Would Garfy make a guest appearance at their show the following week?

"Now, this I like! I'll be most elegant cat in the show," said Garfy as he preened himself in the mirror on the morning of the show. "I am destined for fame," he thought.

\*\*\*

Garfy was in for quite a shock when he got to the show though. Far from being the most elegant, he was afraid he'd look commonplace as he walked into the hall. All the other cats seemed frightfully well-bred and very aloof. It didn't put him off, though. In fact, he was intrigued and excited to be part of all the glitz and glamour. Every cat had their own bed, mostly silk cushions or fine wool blankets. They wore beautiful coloured collars, some of which were even encrusted with diamonds. Everything about these cats was polished, noble and well-mannered.

"Something I know a little bit about myself," said Garfy.

"What was that you said?" came a very refined voice from nearby. Garfy turned to find, sitting on a green silk cushion, being lovingly brushed, a beige and white cat with long fur all about her. She was the most exquisite cat that Garfy had ever seen. Her eyes were half open and her nose was pointing to the air above her, as though she was trying to catch a sniff of supper.

"Sorry," said Garfy, "I was talking to myself."

"Quite a lot of people do around here. They act far above their station too. What did you say your name was?"

"I didn't," said Garfy. He drew himself up, ready for his introduction. "I am Garfield Abercrombie Reginald Fergusson."

"Really?" said the posh cat, "The Fergussons of Cambridge? How wonderful. Well, you must join the show, my dear man. The Fergussons of Cambridge have a long line of winners here at the show."

"Oh, no," said Garfy. "I'm here to make a guest appearance. You might have heard of me and my adventures. It's been all over the news."

"No," said the posh cat, "I haven't, but the Fergussons of Cambridge are legendary in their own right anyway." She stood up in the traditional cat pose of introduction. "My name is Lady Vesper Celeste Tabitha Cavendish. Pleased to make your acquaintance."

Garfy daren't tell Lady Vesper that he hadn't even heard of the Fergussons of Cambridge. He certainly didn't mention that most people called him Garfy. Most undignified! But he was glad he'd met her. She was his kind of cat, sophisticated and elegant; much like himself. These cats were living the life of luxury and Garfy liked the idea of that very much.

"I haven't been entered in one of these shows before. How does it work?" Garfy asked Lady Vesper.

"Well, it's simple really. You must be in tip-top condition, well-groomed and prepared for a long day. Before the show, you must remember to have your ears and eyes cleaned and the sharp bits of your claws trimmed. Your owner *must* bring a top-opening basket and it must have curtains. You'll be judged on your overall body type, eye shape and colour, the quality of your coat and your tail length."

Garfy was glad he had kept training with Uncle Bruno after the problems with Tyson. He was still strong, fit and healthy. There was not much he could do about the length of his tail or the shape of his eyes, however.

"At home, of course," went on Lady Vesper, "we show-cats sleep on velvet or silk cushions, are given the best cuts of meat and are always groomed by someone else. Always try to be groomed by someone else. It is most unbecoming to have to do it yourself."

"Most," said Garfy loftily. He was feeling posher by the minute, just being with Lady Vesper. He could certainly get used to a life of being waited on hand and foot.

Quite a lot of the cat owners at the show knew Garfy and all of them wanted to have their picture taken with him. Garfy practised his most debonair look every time he was snapped. He was thoroughly enjoying being both an elegant *and* a famous cat.

Next day, the pictures of him were all over the internet, on the news and in newspapers and magazines. Garfy had hit the big time. *Everyone* knew him.

\*\*\*

Mrs Paterson watched the comings and goings of the Ely Paterson's cat with great delight. When she saw how well the Ely supermarket was doing – far better than any other supermarket she owned – she simply had to do something to thank Garfy. All Paterson's Superstores had a large foyer before the main shop and Mrs Paterson decided it would be splendid if Garfy were to have his portrait painted and mounted on the wall in the foyer of HIS shop.

Garfy and David thought that was a wonderful idea! A huge portrait was to be created by famous artist Martine Robb. That would keep Garfy on the map for sure. He'd be a household name!

\*\*\*

The day arrived when Garfy was to have his first sitting with Ms Robb. He was up bright and early to be cleaned and groomed by David.

"Just like Lady Vesper said. It is most unbecoming to have to do it yourself."

He was carefully placed in his basket for the journey and, throughout the ride to the artist's studio, Garfy didn't move a muscle for fear of ruining his shiny coat, which was now perfectly smooth and glossy.

When they arrived, they were ushered into a waiting room with a huge window which looked into the artist's studio. There, they could see she was getting ready, pulling out paints and paintbrushes from shelves and drawers, calling to her assistant, "Bring more blue, and water and a large scarf. I'm cold. And while you're about it, brew some coffee and get that large purple silk cushion from the highest shelf in the cupboard. And be quick about it! They're here."

Martine threw open the doors to the waiting room. "Welcome, welcome, welcome!" she called. She strode over to Garfy's basket and peered in. "This must be Garfield Abercrombie Reginald Fergusson! Beautiful! Elegant! Well, we must get started. Quick quick!"

She picked up Garfy's basket and took him to the purple cushion that had been placed in the centre of the studio. "Let's begin, let's begin!" she called to her assistant, who came rushing in with a pile of scarves, a pot of coffee and a boxful of blue paint.

The whole process was fascinating to watch. Martine spent an age looking intensely at Garfy, then making large sweeping marks on the massive canvas she stood at, then back to looking intensely at Garfy again. She called her assistant over several times to bring her something that she needed *right now,* only for it to be discarded as wrong. "No, no, no, this will not do!" shouted Ms Robb. "Wrong brush, wrong paint!" She held her arm out to no one in particular, but the assistant was always there to take away the things she discarded and bring in different paint and different brushes.

"This must be what it's like when you're famous," thought Garfy. "People doing everything you say, running around after you and getting you what you want! That's the life for me!"

***

There were many visits to the studio in the following weeks. Martine became increasingly difficult and her poor assistant became more and more exhausted as the artist's demands became more complicated and particular.

Garfy was stroked and cossetted every few minutes. He was groomed and preened, his cushion was plumped and he was fed the choicest of meat and little delicacies right there on the cushion, so he didn't need to be disturbed.

This pleased Garfy very much but he was beginning to act like Ms Robb. He would turn his nose up at his food if he thought it wasn't the best, so the assistant went out to get more. He wouldn't sit on the cushion until it was plumped up for the hundredth time and he would paw at his fur so he had to be groomed yet again.

"This is what we famous people do, after all," thought Garfy.

\*\*\*

As the painting neared its completion, a writer called Alan came to speak to Garfy and David. He wanted to publish Garfy's autobiography. He wanted to write all about him, interview his friends and follow him around on a typical day.

David was unsure. He could see that Garfy was changing, and not for the better. But Garfy curled himself around Alan and sat on his lap, nose in the air, so he couldn't get up until, reluctantly, David agreed.

And so Alan set about learning all about Garfy.

***

Everyone at Paterson's was really impressed that an author was following Garfy around the supermarket, stopping and making notes every few steps. Garfy sauntered up and down the aisles, showing off his new-found global fame and thoroughly enjoying himself. Alan patted the towels when they arrived at his favourite spot and Garfy curled up for a nap.

He was still there watching when Garfy woke up a while later, ready to follow him wherever he went.

Alan treated Garfy like a prince all the time they were in Paterson's.

The shop assistants watched, a little bemused. They thought it was quite strange that someone was following their Garfy around, treating him like a famous popstar.

The amusement didn't last for long, however. In the weeks that followed, Garfy became more and more demanding and more and more obnoxious. Not satisfied with the leftovers from the deli counter, he insisted on the best cuts from the fresh meat counter. He didn't like the bales of towels any longer either. He sat by them, nose in the air, until someone got a silk cushion from the homewares aisle. He wouldn't even play hide and seek with the children, let alone have anyone stroke and fuss him if they hadn't washed their hands first. The last straw for everyone at Paterson's was when he knocked over the sunglasses stand and attempted to put on the most expensive pair.

Without a word, Hannah, the floor manager, picked up all the fallen sunglasses, took the pair Garfy had on and replaced them on the stand, and turfed the cat into the foyer.

There he sat, under his portrait, looking very aloof. Garfy was used to the high life now, and he wasn't about to stop just because people didn't seem to approve.

Bit by bit, Garfy's friends got fed up with his behaviour. The shoppers at Paterson's stopped putting 'treats for Garfy' on their shopping lists, the children stopped wanting to play hide and seek with him and there certainly weren't any more rides around in their cars.

"Good riddance," thought Garfy. His new celebrity status suited him just fine, thank you very much. Everyone but him began to see that he had become really unpleasant.

Day by day, less and less people stroked Garfy at Paterson's. Most shoppers avoided him as they walked round the shop. Before the newspapers and television, before the cat show and portrait, when Garfy headed over to his favourite spot every day for his snooze there would be plenty of treats waiting for him. But now? Nothing! And there would be no one to stroke him as he settled down for his midday nap.

Garfy began to feel a bit lonely. There didn't seem to be much fun in being a celebrity if there was nobody to share it with.

What could he do to get his friends back?

\*\*\*

Before all the fame, Garfy was known for being friendly. Everyone was pleased to be helped and nuzzled and to have Garfy wind himself around their legs.

So that's what he decided to do: he would go back to being the friendly, elegant cat that everyone at Paterson's loved.

Over the next week, Garfy forgot about his fame and entitlement and just worked on being a friend. He would wake very early, eat his breakfast quickly (he didn't mind what it was) and head out of the cat flap. He didn't wait around to be groomed in front of the mirror; he could do that for himself later. He headed straight to Paterson's, to wait for the delivery lorries. When the first one arrived, Garfy would help to get the cages full of produce to the goods lift. When that was all done, being very careful not to be in the way when the lorry doors shut (another road trip could wait!), he would send them on their way.

"Thanks, Garfy!" the drivers would shout. They only saw him infrequently and, while they had noticed that he hadn't been around as much, they didn't know how badly he'd been behaving. "See you next week!"

The next job was to wait for Hannah to arrive. When she did, Garfy would follow her to her office and sit opposite her, waiting to do anything he could to help.

Hannah tried to ignore Garfy. He had been a royal pain over the last few weeks, thinking he was some kind of celebri-cat. She didn't want to take the time to fuss him any more. Garfy just waited though.

When she screwed up a piece of paper, threw it towards the waste paper basket and missed, Garfy jumped down from the chair, picked it up in his mouth and, standing on his hind legs, dropped it into the basket.

"Slam-dunk, Garfy!" Hannah murmured. She was beginning to warm to him again.

Satisfied that he had done a good job, Garfy was back out in the supermarket and ready to help. He followed the supervisors walking around, making sure everyone had what they needed. He accompanied them when they showed a shopper where a certain item was and he walked beside them when they went to find the price of something for the cashiers.

The evening staff had Garfy keeping them company when they were restocking the shelves. If they dropped anything, Garfy was there to pick it up for them and he gladly pushed all the used packaging all into one pile, so it was easy to pick up and throw into a cage to be taken away.

At night, when the shop was quiet, he wandered through the car park and into the park nearby to bring back presents for everyone. He wanted to show them how much he loved everyone at Paterson's.

It didn't quite have the desired effect. They knew Garfy was trying to be nice but they decided not to swap their sandwiches for fresh mouse for their supper, thank you very much!

As for the shoppers, Garfy made a special effort for them. He miaowed greetings to them as they came in the front door and made sure they had the best trollies and baskets to start their shop. He trotted alongside the trollies and sometimes jumped into them to rearrange the groceries, so nothing got squashed.

He was always happy to see the children. He curled his tail around their legs and purred loudly to get their attention. Then he would spend hours playing hide and seek with them.

Back home, after a long day at Paterson's, Garfy decided that the lavish silk cushion the television crew had bought him as a present for the interview really wasn't for him. He preferred the comfort of David's lap to a scratchy posh bed.

At the weekend, Garfy trotted over to the local park, where he used to play with the children on a big wooden boat with wooden birds perched on the masts. He waited for what seemed like an age.

Just when he thought no one would come – perhaps they'd seen him head down here and didn't want to play with him – Garfy heard the sound of running and laughing.

Round the corner came Morgan and Isabella with a group of their friends, all heading towards the boat and Garfy!

The elegant cat miaowed loudly with delight and ran to greet them.

"Oh Garfy! We have missed you!" Garfy didn't realise until then how much he'd missed them too. "Are you still being a celebri-cat? Or are you coming to play the ship's cat like you used to?" The ship's cat! It reminded Garfy of being at the seaside and all the wonderful things that Salty did for him there.

***

They played all morning in the sun and had the very best time. Garfy enjoyed himself so much more than sitting under his portrait looking aloof. The children took him back into their hearts and Garfy was so happy to have friends again.

The shop assistants and customers at Paterson's took longer to convince though. They were still mistrustful of him and his recent behaviour. What if he turned into the obnoxious celebri-cat again? Treats were definitely off shopping lists for now!

What could Garfy do to convince them that he had turned over a new leaf once and for all?

\*\*\*

The answer came the following Monday when the news reached them that the pet rescue centre on the outskirts of Ely was having to close. The buildings were very old and one of the pipes had burst and flooded the whole place. It was now in ruins. The animals who lived there didn't have a home. Would they end up back on the streets, living as strays again?

A rescue centre nearby had taken them in, but they could only keep them for a little while, as they were full to bursting.

The people of Ely began collecting money in buckets. They organised bingo sessions and summer fairs to raise the amount needed to rebuild the pet rescue centre, but they still had a long way to go.

The reporter on the news said that the shelter needed thousands of pounds. What sad news!

Garfy had been to the centre not so long ago to open a new cat unit. Everyone there had been so nice and all the animals had loved having Garfy, the famous Paterson's cat, there. Even the hedgehogs had uncurled themselves to get a glance at him. But what good was being a celebrity if you couldn't help people who had become your friends? They needed Garfy more than ever, but what could he do?

Garfy walked through the foyer feeling very dejected and unhappy that he didn't seem to be able to help. He walked past his portrait on the wall and looked up at it. He was slightly ashamed of what he had done to everyone in the last few months.

Pretending to be royalty, insisting on the best of

everything, being aloof to everyone – especially the children – hadn't been at all nice.

Garfy took one last look at his portrait as he walked away and secretly wished that it didn't belong to him or Paterson's. He wished they would sell it and get it out of there.

That was it! They could sell the painting!

If Mrs Paterson sold the painting, surely that would raise enough money to save the pet rescue centre?

No sooner had Garfy placed a leaflet for the centre right next to the painting to tell people his idea, the auction had been arranged.

\*\*\*

The auction house was packed the day the painting was due to be sold and a bidding war started very quickly. A smart man in a pinstriped tie and gold glasses was bidding more and more, but someone on the telephone kept bidding against him.

Higher and higher the price rose until, at £10,000, the pinstriped man was beaten by the mystery caller.

An envelope came the very next day, almost like magic. The letter read:

*Dear Mrs Paterson,*

*Please find enclosed the money for the portrait of Garfield Abercrombie Reginald Fergusson. I would be very happy for you to keep it in the foyer at Ely.*

*I'm afraid I don't have much room for it, especially with all the toys I have to store. But I'll be glad to see it when I visit every year in the winter.*

*Yours,*
*FC.*

Garfy was over the moon! He had helped saved the rescue centre and the portrait could stay in Ely too.

He knew all too well the importance of helping out your friends. The silk cushions and expensive sunglasses and sitting with his nose in the air were nothing compared to curling up on warm laps, miaowing his greeting to everyone at Paterson's and playing hide and seek with his friends.

And maybe, in the winter, he would meet this 'FC' person who had bought the painting and thank him personally for putting an end to Garfy's days as a celebri-cat.

# About Garfy

Garfield (aka Garfy) is real and is known as "Ely's most famous cat." In 2012, a new Sainsbury's in Ely was built on the site of an old factory. This was land which had been Garfield's roaming ground previously, so he simply continued to visit. As a result, he has become well known by customers of the supermarket and is something of a local celebrity.

Garfield has his own Facebook page (https://www.facebook.com/The1mrsainsburys) and appears regularly in the local press. He is the 'pin up' cat for the local Cat's Protection, who claim he has saved them over £1000 in cat food because customers at Ely's Sainsbury's donate food because of the 'Garfield factor'.

Garfy has had so many adventures that his owner, David, wanted to create a book to tell Garfy's story more widely. Every one of the stories you read here is based on a real adventure Garfield has had.